MW00527044

THE
TRUNK

KIM RYEO-RYEONG

THE
TRUNK

A Novel

Translated by The Kolab

HANOVER
SQUARE
PRESS

HANOVER
SQUARE
PRESS™

Recycling programs
for this product may
not exist in your area.

ISBN-13: 978-1-335-01501-3

The Trunk

Originally published in Korean in 2015 as 트렁크 by Changbi Publishers, Inc.,
Gyeonggi-do, South Korea.

Hanover Square Press
22 Adelaide St. West, 41st Floor
Toronto, Ontario M5H 4E3, Canada
HanoverSqPress.com

Printed in U.S.A.

1

It was our last night together. The husband had been just the right amount of nice and had kept an appropriate distance. Work would be so much easier if all the husbands were like him. Earlier that day, I had filled the fridge with that Belgian beer he likes. He had one of those kimchi refrigerators and, as it turned out, the drawer was just the right size for beer bottles. The husband had it set to the optimal temperature for "Kimchi taste preservation" and would pull out beers as though he was plucking out radishes from the ground. When I first came to the house, my heart dropped at the sight of the fridge and kitchen shelves stocked full of booze. There were bottles of alcohol everywhere, as though the kitchen had been filled by an alcoholic compulsively storing liquor.

I asked myself why I had even made it to his spouse list in the first place. Did anything in my profile or sample video indicate that I liked to drink a lot? I had mentally prepared myself to ask for an early divorce, even if that meant being punished by the company. It looked like I had stepped in some real shit—just some terrible luck, really. At first, I kept my phone attached to me at all times, so that I could call the rescue team in case the husband got sloshed and started messing around in any way.

Letting first-timers into yearlong marriages without any kind of trial was bad company policy. A colleague of mine once lived with a first-time spouse who hadn't been properly vetted. She was beaten within an inch of her life and had to be rescued. Since the husband was obviously to blame, he received no refund, but my abused colleague was still penalized with a three-month pay cut for the early termination of marriage.

Anyway, fortunately, I never saw any horrible drunken behavior from the husband. He liked to drink, but he didn't overdo it, and his only unusual drinking habit was to impulsively buy more alcohol. At home, the husband usually just had a few of his Belgian beers. Apart from the initial shock of his strange liquor collection, our marriage was smooth sailing.

I had packed all my possessions earlier during the day. My luggage now wasn't very different from what I'd first brought with me when I arrived at the husband's house. I had a few more clothes now, but I'd be throwing out almost everything else. I usually felt a sense of relief throwing things out at the end of a marriage. The only thing I kept as a memento was the wedding ring, which the company gave to couples when they exchanged their wedding vows. All the other little things I used—slippers, a toothbrush, etc.—all went in the trash. If I could, I'd get rid of every little scrap of this marriage.

I looked at the fourteen-karat gold thread ring on my finger. Tomorrow, it would go back into its ring box, along with all memories of the husband. The husband got me as his first wife after he signed up as a member. *Han Jeong-won. Forty years old. A music producer who works under a pseudonym. Never makes media appearances. One-time divorcé.* That was all the information I received. But I was confident it was accurate because the company I worked for, Wedding & Life (or W&L for short), did strict checks before accepting new members.

W&L was an exclusive matchmaking company with a huge reputation—some even said that most singles in Korea felt compelled to sign up. I was a member of New Marriage (NM), W&L's dedicated VIP department. We were given the entire third level of the W&L office. For security reasons, regular employees were unable to access our floor.

While NM was disguised as a department of W&L, it was in fact a secret subsidiary. The vice president of W&L, who happened to be the wife of the CEO, was also the president of NM. Our company had two main pillars around which its operations were centered: the wife team and the husband team. I was a deputy manager in the wife team and worked as a field wife, or FW. Unlike its parent company, NM was not a matchmaking service for single men and women. Instead, NM directly provided clients with a FW or a FH (field husband). As a FW or FH selected to be a client's spouse, we were given the chance to say either yes or no to the assignment. If we replied with no more than three times without justification, we were given the nudge to resign.

Regular W&L employees were quite curious about the identities of these special VIPs that NM catered to separately. While they assumed that we arranged secret marriages for high-ranking officials, überwealthy heirs to large conglomerates, or even princes and princesses from foreign lands, our real business was quite different. But our VIP client list did, in fact, include high-ranking officials, business heirs, and the members of certain elite families, if not royalty. I didn't know how these VIPs found their way to NM. All I knew was that they were definitely unmarried, because the company made sure to verify that, but I was pretty sure they didn't look into who the client was as a person. I was once dropped from consideration for a promotion because I used two of my no's consecutively after an awful marriage with a horrible old man. I only had one no left.

In his bedroom that night, the husband from my current, nearly finished marriage grabbed my hand. I wondered why he had chosen me. How had he even come across NM? But we couldn't just share NM-related information like it were pillow talk; it was strictly prohibited. The company diligently monitored newly inducted members when they entered their first marriage. It was, after all, their first impression of NM, and played an important role in determining future patronage. For that reason, NM assigned neither field wife rookies nor sly, foxlike veterans for first-time clients. Instead, it chose to dispatch experienced, yet not entirely jaded, field wives. If a husband was happy with his experience being my spouse, he would go on to take another field wife.

But if he withdrew from NM after our marriage ended, I would have to write up a report. I made a subtle attempt to probe this husband's intentions.

"Was the marriage okay?"

"Better than expected. You?"

"Same."

So that was that. We both thought it had been a good marriage, so what more was there to say? The awkward silence that followed pushed me to try and continue the conversation.

"By the way, what is that podcast you're doing about? Do your friends even know about it?"

"Well, you know, it's nice to have some things just for myself."

It seemed like the podcast was like a hidden stack of cash for him. He was probably quite happy knowing that it was safely stowed away, so I decided not to push him about it. I didn't want to be the kind of wife who peered under mattresses and felt a sense of triumphant glee when she found the hidden money. Only in such instances did I put the trust between us above all. I didn't want to expose all of the husband's secrets, even if they were just little things. I didn't want to rain on his parade when he was enjoying the thrill and relief of not having been caught yet. I appreciated that he even let me in on the fact that he had such a secret.

The husband climbed on top of me. I could sense that he was eager, but was having trouble getting things started. If he couldn't get it up while sober, maybe he should put some of the alcohol filling the kitchen cupboards to good use, instead of just…mucking around like a limp fish. Anyway, it didn't matter, I could say goodbye now. *Goodbye, have a nice life.*

2

I carefully dragged my suitcase, treading as quietly I could. I wasn't in the mood to deal with Granny, my neighbor from next door. I put it down in front of the door and gently raised the electric key cover to enter the code into the keypad. But before I could even press the remaining digits, Granny stuck her head out.

"You're back?"

"Yes. How have you been?"

"Same as always. You look fairly relaxed, looks like your work trip wasn't too stressful."

I entered the rest of the code and opened the door to step in, Granny in tow. Upon entering, she immediately poured herself a coffee from the commercial coffee dispenser in my kitchen. That darn contraption! But more on that later.

Usually, with most other old ladies in the neighborhood, even little nods hello were awkward, but this granny was unique. When I was in high school, she moved into the neighborhood with her son, and I had been like family to them since. The son and my older brother were the same age, and they soon became friends. Her son spent his college years enjoying passionate romance, and graduated at the same time as his girlfriend, the outline of a baby-bump clear under her gown. Granny always fantasized about the day her son would graduate and bring home paychecks. But just three months after graduating, he brought home a pudgy baby boy instead.

Granny immediately mortgaged out her house and got her son and his wife an apartment opposite hers. Together, the newlywed couple set up a small home office for a business that had nothing to do with either of their degrees. They used their house as storage to sell anything and everything that could be sold online. So, it was only natural that their son was basically left to be raised by his grandmother.

Not much had changed since then. Granny was still busy looking after her grandson. And I had been busy taking care of Granny's coffee needs whenever she came over. She hadn't been visiting as often since about two years ago, when my brother was assigned to work in the

countryside and my parents went along with him. But
now, thanks to that darn coffee dispenser, she came over
so frequently it was like she owned the place.

"Mmm, delicious. Now *that's* coffee," Granny said,
looking approvingly at the coffee dispenser. It never failed
to meet her expectations. By virtue of her double-eyelid
surgery, her eyes looked like they were wide-open in
shock, but she was in fact looking at the coffee dispenser
with a gentle gaze. I did wonder what had possessed the
plastic surgeon to perform their art so boldly. The result
looked as though red semicircles had been etched below
Granny's brow in permanent marker. If you looked a little
closer, you could also see some additional work hidden
at the hairline, the skin pulled taut.

Granny's transformation began ever since the arrival
of the young singer. One day she suddenly started coming home with eggs, tissues, piles of onions or burdock
root. She got all that kind of stuff for free, but then
would pay exorbitantly for ginseng extract, because she
believed it was organic.

The young singer *oppa* was the one selling her these
beliefs and products. He would give her discount coupons every time she went to see him. With the coupons,
Granny had bought a basic electric rice cooker for the
price of a multifunction one, a faulty minifridge at the
price of one that could make and dispense ice, and an

LCD TV for the price of a QLED. *Are these discount coupons, or coupons to pay a premium?* I would wonder. Her son had smashed quite a few such items in fits of rage. If you asked me, he would be better off reselling them online.

Granny liked the young singer oppa. He sang well, danced well, and gave her shoulder rubs. But Granny's son didn't understand why she wasted her time with men like that when she could spend her time with her son instead. What an idiot—what mother would feel her heart race at the sight of her son?

"To him, only his wife is a woman. I'm just a mom until I die," Granny lamented.

The young oppa once gave her an autographed CD, which she proudly showed off. The autograph was so showy and convoluted that I would bet my salary that he himself wouldn't be able to replicate it. Granny and the young oppa had even had dinner together, just the two of them. By a quick estimate, she must have spent a small fortune in goods because of him, with no end in sight. At dinner, the son of a bitch inhaled his expensive eel dish, and then had the audacity to push the bill back toward her. And yet being on that date with him, this man in his forties, made Granny's heart flutter; she loved it. She said it got her blood flowing, without having to take her medication. And so, she continued to see him, and the piles of useless products kept growing on her verandah.

Maybe I should just get her to join NM. That way, she could get a "spouse" without actually remarrying, which her son was dreadfully opposed to. After all, there was always a younger and more attractive field husband ready and waiting to take the young singer oppa's place. NM's fees would be an issue, though. Maybe I should tell her to sell her house. Prices went up when an area was redeveloped, so perhaps I needed to go start a campaign and rally in front of city hall: "The elderly are single and horny! Take responsibility!"

Granny was dreaming about having sex with the young oppa now, but she honestly believed that it would become a reality soon. That's how well he had played his cards; he was a real bastard. Granny had even resorted to borrowing money from my mother to give to him. How could he then pay her back with just lip service?

If I were Granny, I wouldn't have given him a dime until he slept with me. If he wanted the money, *he* should be the one to get naked and take me to bed. After we were done, I'd just hand him a couple of bills and that would be that. But the problem was that Granny was a romantic at heart. Maybe NM needed to reduce its rates and help make contract marriages more commonplace.

"You were pretty popular back in the day, weren't you?" I asked Granny.

"I was."

"What would you do on dates back then?"

"We'd do what people do now—there isn't much else for grown-ups to do for fun. We'd have a drink, then get into bed with each other."

People gossiped about Granny, calling her a pitiful widow when she was single and, when she wasn't, talking about her like she were the kind of person to try and fish for any man who caught her eye. They had something to say about every outfit she wore, and would criticize her makeup too. "Who are you trying to impress by looking like that?"

People were going to chatter no matter what, so Granny decided to give them something to *really* talk about. She led a life so full of steamy romance, she made those busybodies regret not being widows themselves. Love and affection between two people may not be easy to spot when they're married, but it's hard to miss when they're dating. When people saw flowers being delivered to her place, or Granny getting all dolled up for a date after work, they realized that she went through different dates like she was going through the seasons.

Granny's colleague had once grumbled to her, "When

I get home from work, I'm so done with everything, I don't even feel like getting it on. Props to you, honestly."

Granny set her colleague's nether regions on fire by responding, "You feel like that because when you get home from work, all you have waiting for you is your old ball and chain. It's different when you have a lover."

While a fun anecdote, I was suddenly confused about whether she was talking about the past or the present. Could it be that the "lover" she mentioned was the young oppa? Maybe he was actually in love with this senior femme fatale. He had eel on their date, maybe because he knew it was an aphrodisiac. What a thoughtful, hardworking little piece of shit.

"You're at your prime. Meet plenty of guys now so that you don't have any regrets later," Granny told me. "I've gotta go now. Jun-soo will be back soon."

Granny poured two hot drinks from the dispenser—coffee with milk and Yulmu millet tea. Her grandson, Jun-soo, really liked tea, so Granny took a cup for him whenever he came home. The coffee would be for the bus driver, who dropped Jun-soo off. When Granny finally left, I came to a decision. I was going to throw away that damn coffee dispenser once it ran out of stock, no matter what. The reason I even had it in the first place was my friend Shi-jeong.

Last year, Shi-jeong had decided that she was going to

become a webtoon creator, and had started taking classes from a manhwa artist. Shi-jeong could not do her creative work at home, because her parents were opposed to her becoming an artist. And so, she came up with a plan. She would first focus on getting her own studio space. After that, she would participate in and win some webtoon contests. Then, she would use that success to convince her parents that being a manhwa artist was a viable career. For the time being, however, she still needed a studio to work in.

When Shi-jeong showed me some of her work, I thought she had real potential. I also thought that aspiring to start afresh so close to thirty was quite brave. So, I lent her the generous, but not too generous, sum of five hundred thousand won. At the time, we were twenty-eight and the anxiety and anticipation around turning thirty was huge. The money was my way of sending support to the thirty-year-old Shi-jeong of the future.

What I had forgotten, however, was that Shi-jeong often got caught up in some deep, inexplicable sentimentality and developed new passions with worrying frequency. She went back and forth between interests like some crazy bitch on a seesaw. Damn thirty was right in front of us, so it made sense.

To no one's surprise, the studio did not last long. Shi-jeong watered the plant I gifted her on opening day a couple of times, and that was it.

The space she had rented was in a building near the subway station in Seoul's corporate hub, Yeoksam-dong. Such spaces were usually prime real estate, but Shi-jeong had paid a ridiculously low deposit for her studio. The trade-off was a high monthly rent, which she couldn't afford, so she was out in six months. Shi-jeong hadn't even arranged for a place to store her stuff: she had just left the studio, maintenance charges unpaid, like a criminal fleeing a crime scene. She had been generous with her money when it came to things like buying a big coffee dispenser, so it was ridiculous to me that she was being so defiant when it came to maintenance charges. News flash—Shi-jeong herself couldn't even drink coffee. If she had any, she spent the rest of the day in the bathroom. In any case, what use would a novice artist have for all that coffee in a studio that rarely saw any clients?

Anyway, Shi-jeong closed her studio and brought the coffee dispenser to my house. She told me that she'd definitely pay me back the money I had lent her, and I should think of the coffee dispenser as collateral. She talked about the machine like it was some kind of revolutionary innovation. *It's super easy to clean, and there's no need to bother with boiling water—one simple press of a but-*

ton and the machine gives you coffee! You would think she'd brought over a coffee robot or something.

I had never asked for collateral in the first place, and the whole idea of giving someone an industrial-sized coffee dispenser to put in their home seemed like a very manhwa-esque way of thinking. The machine had three buttons: milk coffee, black coffee, and tea. The webtoon dream suited her, and I thought that she should keep it going. I tried to tell her as much.

"You can use the machine later when you have a studio again."

"Oh, I'm only going to draw as a hobby now," was her response.

So that was how I ended up with a coffee dispenser in my home. Shi-jeong was a warm and decisive person, but her problem was that she was simple, just like a three-buttoned coffee dispenser.

3

I wished I had a small house somewhere in a tranquil forest. It would be nice to live alone, with minimal housekeeping and tableware, spending my time leisurely painting the walls and floors. I wondered out loud if I could find a quaint little house like that somewhere, but my earnest dream was apparently uninspiring to Shi-jeong.

"There are a lot of abandoned houses in the mountains if you look for them. If you're lucky, you might just find someone willing to rent one out to you. Finding a house isn't your biggest problem, though. A woman living alone in the forest draws attention. If someone were to visit you, and you welcomed them in, then they'd probably come to bother you all the time. It's just something bad waiting to happen."

Couldn't you just call the cops? I thought. Although, come to think of it, NM rescue teams called to help FWs rarely made it before serious harm had already been inflicted. It looked like my dream of living in a small forest house, where I hung laundry in the yard and took long naps on the deck, would have to remain just a dream. Here I was, only twenty-nine, but already so worn-out.

"Hey, Inji," Shi-jeong said, "if a man doesn't call, what does it mean?"

"He's not interested."

"What if he's just shy?"

Men could be in the middle of getting brain surgery, but if they liked you, they would still call. Shy? Yeah, right. Love let you overcome that sort of thing. It seemed like the guy she was talking about was someone she used to draw webtoons with. They apparently stopped talking when she gave up on that dream. If that was the case, then he was just a friendly colleague, at most.

I told her that if she had any lingering feelings for him, *she* should make the call and coax him into bed, but that just made her all flustered. She took the joke too seriously. I didn't get why Shi-jeong was like that about sex. It was as if she'd been whacked over the head while doing the deed or something, making her feel weird and embarrassed about the act itself. Thinking of love and sex as so directly connected seemed so outdated to me. Only some country bumpkin would think like that. It was natural to want to be intimate and physical with someone when you loved them. Things just became awkward otherwise.

"I'm not like that. Are you only dating to get laid?" fumed Shi-jeong.

"It's more like I go on dates with people, and we just end up sleeping together. You always go to the movies on dates, right? It's not because you're in love with popcorn, is it? If that was the case, then you should've bought a popcorn maker instead of that lousy coffee dispenser! Look, if you wanna be a nun, so be it."

"Are you incapable of seeing relationships as something more than that?"

"Look at the guy next door. He slept with his wife a few times, and now they even have a kid together."

"I can't talk to you if you're gonna be like this."

"Girl, just take your coffee dispenser and go."

Shi-jeong did not take the coffee dispenser. Instead, she sent me another unwanted gift—a thin, pasty man named Om Tae-seong. While he wouldn't be my first choice, he wasn't too bad. I was told he was a "breath of fresh air," who was supposedly going to reeducate me on relationships and show me that men and women could do more than just have sex with each other.

Usually, when a marriage contract came to a close, I had to fill out a marriage report and then I got a week off to relax. However, thanks to Granny and Shi-jeong, I didn't get a moment's rest. Last time it was her webtoon-writing colleague, and now this guy... Why was I being roped into all this?

"I heard you work at W&L," Tae-seong said on our date.

"Yup."

"So even W&L employees go on blind dates."

"Yeah, I guess. Anyway, how do you know Shi-jeong?"

"We met at a workshop on home-made *tteok*."

Tteok? She was making rice cakes now? She changed hobbies *again*?

"Did you know you can even make *injeolmi* using a rice cooker? You just need to pound the rice after cooking it."

He seemed pretty serious about his tteok hobby. He said that he had a variety of handmade tteok at home. I had never, in my entire life, heard anyone brag about their tteok collection. What was I supposed to make of this strange thirty-three-year-old guy and his love for tteok? He even wore a rainbow-colored tteok-patterned tie to the pasta place we were meeting at.

I'm sorry, is this some sort of prank? I wanted to ask him.

Such a pure and virtuous love for tteok—to think that it wasn't sex but rice cakes that brought a man and woman together. He seemed like he would be a good match for Shi-jeong, so I couldn't understand why he was here, sitting in front of me. I really couldn't care less about him.

Tae-seong wanted to show me some tteok cake, which he insisted was in no way inferior to regular cake, so he ended up dragging me to a tteok café in the charming neighborhood of Insa-dong. It was right across from an art gallery that I always made sure to avoid. In fact, I had a bad feeling about the whole thing from the moment we got into the taxi, and Tae-seong told the driver to take us to Insa-dong. Today was really not my day.

Insa-dong was where it all started with NM. I was still in college but graduation was fast approaching, and I had secured a job interview with a publisher in Anguk-dong. The manager asked a series of questions, none of which seemed even remotely related to the actual job.

"Do you like to drink?"

"Occasionally," I replied. Occasionally was unlikely to be enough. There were several breweries nearby, and I was well aware that most of their alcohol ended up at the publisher's.

"What do you like to drink, Ms. Noh?" inquired the manager.

"I like beer."

"Oh yeah, beer's good. I had a good feeling about you from the moment I saw your résumé. I like your name. Anyway, thanks for coming along today. I'll let you know whether it's a yes or a Noh in the next few days. Ha ha ha."

That was how the interview went. It seemed like my fate had been decided with my name when I was born, and I was destined to always have to wait for a yes or a no. After the interview, I made my way to Insa-dong with an empty feeling in my chest. I spotted an art gallery and decided to go in and warm up. The gallery was hosting an international art expo, and I started to take a look around. I was moving through the hall, comparing the works with those on the pamphlet I had purchased at the entrance, when a woman approached me.

"Good art, isn't it? The play on perspective is interesting," she remarked.

The piece was a canoe made of metal rulers. It was named *Time* but, being the layperson I was, I couldn't really connect the title to the piece without an explanation. The woman looked like the intellectual type, and seemed like someone affiliated with the exhibit. I was embarrassed. Why did she have to approach me of all people? *The play on perspective is interesting*—sure, I guess, what did I know?

"I don't quite know. I just saw it as a boat," I mumbled.

"It is indeed a boat."

The woman smiled gently, and moved to a different piece of art. I tried to continue looking around but, for some weird reason, I kept feeling bothered by her presence, so I left the exhibition after only a hurried inspection. Just as I had descended the stairs of the gallery, the woman called out to me. Something about it was unsettling. I didn't want to make conversation with a complete stranger, especially not one who I couldn't put my finger on in the slightest. She had the elegant airs of a woman who could make cheap taffy look and taste like fine chocolate. And she made me uncomfortable.

I had this strong urge to run up to the group of Japanese tourists who had just come in, and try to join them. If they asked me what on earth I was doing, I'd just beg them to save the questions until we had moved far away from that weird gallery lady.

I pretended that I couldn't hear her calling out to me, and just kept walking. I heard the click-clack of her heels as she rushed down the stairs. The woman lightly grabbed on to my arm. *Damn it.*

"Yes?" I inquired.

"Did you have a job interview today, by any chance? Let's have a cup of tea."

She must have known from my typical interview outfit. It wasn't like my entire life was ruined if I didn't find a job ASAP and yet, she had me hooked with the word *interview*. We went to the teahouse next to the art museum. I knew nothing about art, but still followed her lead, as if bewitched.

The woman pulled out a business card. It was embossed with the W&L logo and said Marriage Consulting Agency. I remembered once hearing that W&L's clientele included a lot of highly qualified and good-looking people. Some students from my college had already signed up as members.

I didn't know what to say to the woman. I accepted the business card out of courtesy, with no real intention of signing up for the service. I later found out that the wife of the W&L CEO ran the art gallery.

"Thank you," I said. "I'll think about signing up for your services and get back to you."

"I am offering you a job with the company," she clarified, proceeding to a barrage of questions.

"Are you graduating this year?"

"Yes, I am."

"And your major?"

"Korean language and literature."

"Are you conversational in any other languages?"

"I went to Japan as an exchange student."

"Do you like any sports?"

"Baseball."

"What team do you go for?"

"The Doosan Bears."

"The K-Series this year must have been quite disappointing for you then."

The Bears had suffered a four-game losing streak that year, yielding the Korean Series championship to the SK Wyverns. Their performance the previous year had been the exact same. A four-game loss was really fucking hard to swallow. That year, I got mad during the games, then got mad again watching the highlight reels, and then ended up binging beers like never before. I think I set a personal record for beer consumption that year. The fucking Bears, they really had to get their shit together.

This woman, whom I had disliked from the beginning, was now interviewing me more seriously than the publisher from earlier that day had. She was like one of those religious people who ran after you because you had a "spiritual energy." It was awkward and unpleasant. I said I needed more time to think, and immediately fled.

Long story short, that publishing company ended up saying no and I wasn't hired. Most of my classmates failed to secure work too, so it wasn't a huge blow to my pride. It definitely wasn't ideal either, but I thought I could take up the offer to work at W&L, and then change jobs as soon as something better came along. My senior classmates had been telling me that switching to something else once you already had a job was far easier than getting a job in the first place.

When I reached out to her, the woman from the gallery enthusiastically agreed to meet me again. That was the day I learned that the woman was actually a scout for potential NM employees. When she told me about the field wife concept, I wasn't really surprised. Or maybe, I was so shocked that I couldn't process any emotion.

Contract spouses—what on earth? I remember thinking. FWs were just escorts, but with insurance and a high salary. This was institutionalized prostitution. *Fuck, why have I been picked for this? Is that the sort of impression I gave her?* I even considered reaching out to a journalist friend of mine to say that I had discovered a juicy story. If the story got some attention, I could maybe even get a gig out of it. "Breaking news! A dark secret hidden under the promise of love! Matchmaking company revealed to be escort service!"

"To be absolutely clear, we are not an escort service," the woman insisted during our meeting. "We have clients who aren't looking for sex, and even some who are physically unable to have sex. They're just people who want to have a slightly unorthodox marriage."

"Well, then, you could just match them with one another," I pointed out.

"Just because they're similar people doesn't mean they

will get along with each other. They spend good money and need guaranteed results."

"Why was I scouted?"

"You're attractive, but you don't seem like you could ever be a prostitute."

The type of woman who wants to get married at least once. According to the gallery woman, that was the category I fell under. So, this was the world we lived in, one where even spouses could be rented. W&L charged NM members a high annual subscription and a matrimonial fee and, in return, offered them a selection of spouses. It was like the spouses were luxury personal items, like a Dior perfume or a Birkin bag. I had somehow ended up in a world in which I knew nothing, and where more and more unknowns appeared at every turn.

Snapping out of my memories of that day at the gallery, I glanced over at Insa-dong beyond the window. It had been a while since I'd come here, but nothing had really changed. There was a restaurant where there used to be a pharmacy, and a café where there used to be a restaurant, but the atmosphere of the place was the same as always. Calm yet bustling. I did not want to stay there any longer.

"I'm sorry, I didn't know this was going to be a date," I told Tae-seong.

"You heard that I'm unemployed and it put you off, right?"

"No, I just don't have the time to be seeing anyone right now."

"Twenty-nine is a bit too old to play hard to get. Let's just see where this goes."

What on earth was up with this guy? Not even a part-time job to his name and here he was, talking a big game. Maybe he had a big trust fund or something. In that case, he should get straight to setting up his own tteok shop. Shi-jeong herself should have taken that pure heart of hers and gone out with him herself. Why the hell would she set *me* up with this bastard who went around with his hair parted like the Red Sea?

"You looked nervous, Inji, so I said that as a joke. You know, sometimes people say you're too old to be picky, right? Don't listen to those people. They're the sort of people who have no substance, like hollow bread. I'm the real deal, a man with tenacity and a full heart, like a rice cake."

Yeah, well what about baram-tteok? Isn't that rice cake with a bunch of air in the middle? I almost replied.

"How much do you make? Deputy manager at twenty-nine? You've done well."

"Was that also a joke?"

"No, I asked because I was genuinely curious. The

job market is volatile at the moment. Being a deputy manager at twenty-nine is impressive. And full-time too, I presume?"

"I'm going to leave now, my apologies."

I stood up with the bill. I always paid when I wanted to end unpleasant meetings. I didn't want to eat food bought by a man I didn't like, or become the kind of woman who used dates as an excuse to sponge off of people.

"You paid for dinner earlier. I can get this," I said.

"Really? Honestly, I did think we would split the bill at the pasta place earlier, since it was so expensive. Ha ha ha. Yes, that *was* a joke."

You wanna hear a joke? You're so pasty, you look like you covered your face in tteok powder. What nerve. I hadn't asked him to pay for dinner; he was the one who had rushed to get his wallet out. I felt exhausted. I held my card out to the server.

Shi-jeong came over the next day with some green tea and homemade tteok. She made the tteok with a steamer, but it was nothing special. Shi-jeong didn't really have any outstanding talents, but she was good at anything she tried her hand at. Her problem was that she always gave up before making it to pro level. Her cake was exceptionally good for a homemade one, but I didn't know if I would feel the same if I'd paid for it.

"Wait, so, you cut your date short?"

"Tae-seong is too much of a character, trying to get to know him felt exhausting."

"Why are you being like that? He's nicer than you think."

"If you have to *think* someone is nice, they are not."

"Isn't he cute, though?"

"Cute, how?"

I didn't know where Shi-jeong was getting the "nice, friendly vibe" from. I was sure that if there had been any chemistry between us, he would have beelined to a motel—that's the kind of guy he was. Someone needed to hand him something to cover up that raging boner of his.

Dating people was so hard. Sometimes, I just wanted to quit my job at W&L and sign up to be a client instead. I envied how flexible things were for them. They could select spouses based on their own specific preferences, and marry them for a specific amount of time. These weren't lifelong commitments, so they could get as specific as they wanted. I knew a senior colleague in her fifties who had members seek her out even after she retired. Her clients found comfort with her, so they would go to her when they wanted a bit of a break between marriage contracts, as if taking a sabbatical. For her, it was like seasonal, fixed-term employment.

At this point in my life, I had worn four wedding rings, but I still didn't understand men. They seemed to have as many personalities as they had sperm. The more I tried to get to know them, the less I seemed to understand. But whenever I would start to give up, I'd suddenly see a glimmer of hope, only to be let down again. When I saw a guy like Tae-seong, who seemed typical but also extremely atypical, it frustrated me to no end. Shi-jeong must have been bribed with tteok or something. She kept sugarcoating Tae-seong.

"You should give him another chance. He's got a certain innocence to him, even if it isn't immediately obvious."

"I like guys who have a certain passion in them, especially when it isn't obvious. Sorry, Shi-jeong, but I start working tomorrow and I really need to get a few things ready."

"All right, that's fine."

Shi-jeong left with coffee from the dispenser. I heard her voice outside a bit later.

"Granny! Granny, are you home? I have coffee for you."

"Come in, come in."

The amount of meddling in other people's business

that took place around here. Shi-jeong and Granny's relationship, formed by fate in the form of a coffee dispenser, was so precious, truly, it brought tears to my eyes. Shi-jeong would probably dine with Granny, and I would probably be invited to join. Then, Shi-jeong would come back to my place for coffee. How in the world did I escape from this vicious cycle propagated by the coffee dispenser? Granny took even toilet paper from the young oppa without question, but refused to take the fancy dispenser I was so willingly offering her. *Please, Granny, rid me of this machine.* I made a silent plea.

4

I walked through the main gate, my staff ID around my neck. The first floor contained a lobby and meeting room, the second floor was mainly occupied by W&L, and the third floor was home to NM. I scanned my ID card via the terminal to my left, where NM staff needed to go through one more entrance to get into the office. Upstairs, the initials *NM* were gilded in large letters on the tempered glass doors.

As I entered, I saw the wife team workstations to the left. I made eye contact with the director, who was sitting by the tea table, pouring a cup of coffee. She was considered the leading commander of the FW team, but had no experience as a FW herself. She never put on any airs about rank, and used the same workspace as everyone else. She offered me a coffee, which I happily accepted.

I saw Manager Park wave her hand to me in greeting. The office always seemed the same, no matter when I visited. There were a few rookie FWs who I hadn't met yet, but this was nothing unusual. It was entirely possible that I wouldn't recognize these new FWs even if we were to cross paths on an assignment. Today, there was a particularly large number of people out of the office.

I chose a desk by the window. FWs who did a lot of field-work did not have designated desks, instead using any available workspace within a section of the floor that had been set aside for them. I switched on the computer and glanced at the hyacinth next to the monitor. The blue flower bloomed alluringly, in all its artificial, plastic glory. There were no real flowers at NM, since the desks were empty most of the time. The director placed a cup of coffee on my desk and dragged a chair over.

"I saw your report. Looks like business this time was uneventful," said the director.

"Yes, it was. Nothing new in the office, is there?"

"Nothing new? What do you mean? Our sweet little Ms. Yoo has been eating for two."

Assistant Manager Yoo In-young had been with the company for almost two years. Employees got promoted rather quickly in the early stages at NM, in order to match the high base salary of regular W&L employees. The ones who passed screening after six months of probation were directly promoted to assistant manager.

Anyway, long story short, Yoo got pregnant on her very first assignment. Whether or not she kept the child was up to her, but she would have to inform the husband of her decision. Unfortunately, clients rarely wanted to keep the baby, and most FWs felt the same way, so they usually got an abortion. Yoo's husband was no different, and had no desire to keep the baby. However, Yoo did. In cases like these, the company would smooth things over with the husband, and pay the FW a fixed amount of child support until the child reached adulthood. It was a form of severance pay for them, since they had to stop working due to their pregnancy, and also a measure to curb any unwanted backlash later.

The issue was that Yoo's husband was quite adamant about not keeping the baby. Yoo was left with no choice but to have it behind his back. Apparently, she was quite confident that she'd be able to continue working as a FW, while raising her child on the side. It was sweet but, ultimately, naive. Did Yoo think that she could just keep being married to the same husband? Who would look after the baby if she was assigned a different spouse? I had never seen a member request a FW with a baby, and I doubted that was going to change anytime soon.

"When Yoo found out she was pregnant, she bought cake to celebrate."

"She must have been happy about the news. And then really heartbroken by the husband's response."

"A single daydream can bring a lifetime of suffering. Once you're settled in, come to my desk. I printed out a list of security companies."

"Okay."

I took a sip of my coffee, which had been freshly brewed. I realized that it tasted too smooth. It was missing that unpleasant, lingering taste that you get from instant coffee. Apparently the coffee dispenser had grown on me.

I started my day by updating the virus software on my computer, as well as a bunch of other updates, since the computer had been left untouched for so long. Then I made a routine call to a FW who was on an assignment. I asked about her well-being using the standard code. "Would you like to subscribe to our newspaper?"

"I already have a subscription to a different newspaper," she replied.

This response meant that everything was fine. If they had responded, *What do you offer as a service?* I would have marked it down. That kind of a response was a request to monitor the situation, implying potential problems. If the FW replied, *If I sign up for a newspaper subscription, do I also get sports newspapers for free?*, that meant there had been some kind of violence. And if a call did not connect three times in a row, we sent out a rescue team.

Problematic members usually showed their true colors within about three months of marriage. They usually couldn't hide their true nature for longer than that. I remembered one instance where the FW would have died if the rescue team hadn't shown up when they did. There had been no response from her, despite repeated calls. On the other hand, when we called the husband, he immediately picked up his phone and sounded oddly calm. This set off alarm bells, and the rescue team was dispatched. They found the FW in an extremely precarious situation. She had been robbed of all her belongings and locked in a room, unable to call for help. Thankfully, there didn't seem to be any such harrowing situations today.

Rescue services at NM were provided by a private security company. To people outside the company, they were known as a service working through W&L to provide married couples crisis response in cases of domestic violence. The contract with the regular security company was set to expire that year, and the feedback from employees had been that they were too slow to respond, so W&L was in the process of vetting other companies to replace them.

Oddly enough, however, the rescue team wasn't called for too often. This didn't mean that all contract marriages were happy ones, just that members knew they would be able to switch spouses soon enough, so they usually decided to just save their energy and bear with it until the contract ended. Sometimes that meant sleeping in different rooms, but that was easier than filing complaints or requesting a new spouse.

I realized that it was lunchtime, and I should probably get something to eat. I scanned the room, searching for someone to accompany me, when my eyes met with Manager Park's. I texted her to go grab lunch, but she was busy finishing up a chart and couldn't come. *Why is she working so hard on some dumb chart?* I thought.

Then I heard the director call me to have lunch with her. I couldn't believe I would have to spend my lunch break with my boss. Maybe I could try dragging Park along. Did people really have to take their jobs so seriously? *Well, guess it's up to me to go entertain the director. Honestly though, how do I always end up having lunch with her whenever I come to the office?*

I grabbed my bag. The director was waiting with the door open for me. We were heading to the elevators when we bumped into Deputy Manager Kim, a field husband with the company. It had been almost two years since I last saw him.

"Kim, it's nice to see you. How long has it been?"

"I was away on a job for two years."

"Where to?"

"Beijing—the ex-wife runs a study-abroad consultancy there."

"Are you heading out to lunch? Come join us, if you don't have plans already."

"Sure." Thank heavens, I had been saved. I was no longer stuck going to a one-on-one meal with only the director, and had been spared from having to join in on rants about in-laws I'd never met, or children I had no interest in knowing. Now that I had Kim with me, my work was cut down by half.

Kim entered the company two years before I did. I met him right after I finished fieldwork training, before starting work as a trainee. Us trainees were responsible for taking care of things at the office for FWs who were out in the field. At the time, I was in a supporting role for a senior staff member from the wife team. They were planning a strategy where members could rent out a residence straight from NM during their contract with us. We needed a lot of capital to make this work. Even if we created an NM Town, it was unlikely our members would live there, since most of them were quite particular about maintaining their privacy.

Kim was working on the same project, but on the husband team. In the end, it was deemed too risky to buy houses and rent them out. Instead, if a member wanted, we could contract a residence for them through an NM representative. That was safe. Once a member deposited the rent, we would secure a place via W&L. That way, we could protect the client's privacy and avoid messy problems for NM too. Very roughly, that's what the whole project was about. I went back and forth between the husband and the wife teams, relaying documents and, in the process, got close to Kim.

He was the only senior coworker I felt comfortable around, but he wasn't actually my senior anymore. I still looked up to him as a mentor-like figure, but we now shared the same level in terms of corporate hierarchy, thanks to his rebellious spirit. Kim had a habit of dragging the company's hushed-up issues and controversies out from the shadows and into the open for us all to see and address. He had also been excluded from promotions as disciplinary action for terminating marriages midcontract. It was like he was trying to make sure he was still just a deputy manager when he retired at a ripe old age.

"Why do rich people bother choosing these kinds of marriages?" I once asked him.

"It's much more of a hassle to break up with someone once you're married legally than if you're just a couple living together through NM. Unless your spouse has some kind of extreme problem, it's not easy to get a divorce. And beyond the legalities, what could be a bigger problem than hating the person you live with? Once their cute, pudgy feet start looking like bear paws, that's when the torture begins. These people want to be free from the cycle of getting together with someone only to then inevitably break up. When you think about it that way, it's pretty logical, but it also feels a bit cold and heartless."

"It's voluntary misogamy," I pointed out.

"Or it's that they just didn't meet anyone they thought was worth proposing to, with the risks and all," he responded. "Most people who oppose marriage have been married themselves. They get into the system but, once they're in there, realize that it sucks. How many such people do you think actually quit their marriage? I'm not blaming those who don't. It's more exhausting to flee a marriage and deal with the aftermath than to simply stay in it and keep it going. Life just goes on."

"Are couples that actually grow old together some kind of divine miracle then?"

"I don't know. It's probably just that one thing leads to another, and they end up growing old together, don't you think? Ha. Anyway, if all couples stuck together, our job would be in danger."

"I wasn't sure you'd be suited for this job. Has it been all right for you?" I asked Kim.

"The job's perfect for me. It's fun," he replied.

In our profession, we occupied a space in our client's lives that existed somewhere between that of a lover and a wife. I regretted it from the start, and would regret it in the end, but breaking out of the cycle when I was stuck inside it felt impossible. Calling it surrender would make me seem too pitiful, and calling it faith seemed... strangely cowardly. Like a car stuck in a rut, its wheels struggling against the mud, I knew that I would manage to get out eventually. It was just a matter of having patience and keeping the engine running.

"If you ever go to Beijing, let me know," Kim said. "I'll map out the best restaurants for you. There's this restaurant that does great lamb *shabu shabu*, and they even do your nails while you wait."

My stomach rumbled just hearing about Chinese food.

Then, I spotted him. Om Tae-seong, wearing his damn rainbow rice cake tie, holding a cake box, right in front of the office entrance.

I tried to hide behind Kim as we walked out, only for Tae-seong to loudly call out my name. *Oh, he's a real fucking bastard.* I pretended not to hear him. Tae-seong walked over to us with a big, stupid smile dancing on his face. I could not believe that he was doing this right outside my workplace; it was beyond humiliating.

The director, probably at least slightly charmed by his fair and pleasant appearance, greeted him with a polite smile. She turned to me and asked, "Would you like us to go ahead and leave you two to catch up?"

"No, that's all right." I turned to Tae-seong. I had no choice but to take him along. "Why don't you come along with us?"

The seafood restaurant we went to was pretty popular and known for its good food. It was already crowded, and we didn't get a table immediately. During the whole time we waited, Tae-seong chattered at me like we had been dating for a thousand years. He went on and on about the state of some seafood place near the beach, the difference between charcoal briquettes and charcoal fire, comparing fish dried by the ocean air and by a food dehydrator, what restaurant served which sides—it was never-ending. *Please, just shut up*, I begged internally.

Finally, when a waiter came to us, we asked to be seated in pairs. Tae-seong and I were seated some distance from the director and Kim's table. Right until we sat down, Tae-seong kept going on about how we had to make sure to make a reservation next time. The restaurant didn't even take reservations.

I didn't think he was a bad person per se, but for

some reason, every single word he said just pissed me off. I was sick of these meaningless and, frankly, pointless meetings. I decided that I would just have to make him lose all interest in me by becoming a foul-mouthed, abhorrent woman who made his pasty skin crawl. My method would be concise and direct, like well-written prose. This was going to end today in just four steps: setup, buildup, confrontation, and resolution. I took a moment to think as I chewed the seasoned seaweed side dish. Tae-seong picked up his chopsticks.

"That's your lanyard, right? I wish I had one…"

If you want one so badly then just go look at the office bulletin board, they often advertise job openings there. The setup.

"I've heard you have to be well-qualified to have access to the third floor. My little sister worked briefly for W&L, but got frustrated when they told her to pick up her game. Her small monthly paycheck probably didn't help. But she did say that not just anyone could make it to the third floor. You must be more skilled than I thought."

More than you thought? The buildup.

"And having talked to Shi-jeong, it's not like you're not interested in me at all. I mean, I'm pretty okay-looking, and I'm quite capable, so there's really no reason for you *not* to like me. Playing hard to get won't make you any more attractive at this point, so let's just give it a go."

This son of a bitch. I gestured for him to come closer. The confrontation.

"When someone tells you something, shouldn't you at least try and get it through your thick skull? Do you *want* to get hit in the face? Go and tell Shi-jeong that if she's gonna keep running her mouth, I'm gonna wring her fucking neck, got that? As for you, what do you mean 'capable'? Not only are you incompetent, you're also a pain in the fucking ass. If you don't have a job, just stay at home and pound your 'tteok' in silence, yeah? The *hand*made way."

I took my plate and moved over to where my colleagues were sitting. *The resolution.*

5

I thought that would be enough. I honestly believed that I had gotten rid of him by showing him just how terrible I could be. And yet, Tae-seong had been showing up in front of my office building every day for the past week.

He didn't say anything to me, probably in the hopes that I would reach out to him first. He seemed to wholeheartedly agree with the old Korean saying that women are like trees—come at them ten times and even the mightiest will fall for you. If I could, I would axe that saying. Whether a tree falls depends, in the end, on the tool being used. If you reject a person more than ten times only to then give in and say yes, is that not just surrender? Can a love that comes from defeat really be a happy one? I would rather have my head chopped off with an axe.

Tae-seong was a source of concern for the director, who thought that he was attracting too much attention. Employees at W&L would get a bit too interested in people's relationships, which was just a curse that came with the job. The folks on the second floor were probably wondering who the guy with the rice cakes was looking for. Generating too much curiosity wasn't a good idea, as it could start creating problems for you at NM.

Nothing good came out of other people in NM recognizing you. You never knew when or where you might be sent for fieldwork. Imagine meeting your new neighbor and realizing it was your coworker—you definitely wanted to avoid that. Lately, I had been noticing people giving me those quick, curious glances. Tae-seong's good looks were also adding to their curiosity. It got to the point where the director asked me if the company needed to step in and resolve the issue, but I insisted that I would take care of it myself.

I stood looking at Tae-seong for a little while. He was standing at the front gate and, as always, holding a tteok cake. What was it about him that made me so uncomfortable? From our very first meeting, I had always sensed there was something off about him, but I just wasn't sure what. I couldn't quite put my finger on it. Even after we had parted, I couldn't shake the feeling that I had just narrowly escaped something.

Tae-seong worked tirelessly to make tteok cakes every day, even though he knew they wouldn't be accepted. Showing up with a gift every day sounded like a romantic gesture, so why did it give me the creeps? Every morning, Tae-seong would sieve rice flour, steam the tteok into cake form, and then neatly put everything into a box. To me, it felt like he was sharpening knives every morning to put in a box and give to me. Hating someone really put all kinds of horrible ideas in your head. I needed to get out of this as soon as possible. It did not benefit either of us to keep this up, so I approached Tae-seong.

"Inji, are you free today?" he asked.

"Let's talk," I responded.

We went to the café across the road from W&L, and I ordered two Americanos. I wasn't in the mood to be nice and ask him what he liked, so I just went ahead with what I wanted. I took the coffees, went to a corner seat, and placed the drinks in front of him. I wasn't there to beat around the bush, so I got straight to the point.

"My company's been keeping an eye on you."

"Well, since it's a dating agency, I guess we'll be paired up soon."

I stared at Tae-seong in silence. What was this, some

kind of proposal? Tae-seong was fair, and he had nicely shaped features. He had the face of a rich boy next door, or the secure heir to a fortune of old money. But he didn't live up to those good looks. He would really benefit from just keeping his mouth shut. When he opened his mouth, his true colors came to light, so he really needed to just wear a mask or something to cover it up. You could tell that he knew he was good-looking, and it probably made life so easy for him. I was sure he used that face of his to disarm guarded women, the way geniuses use their intelligence to solve complex calculus. Pretty privilege was very much real. It was obvious why he kept coming back to me, even though I was so resistant.

His sister used to work at W&L, but what he had learned from her about the company must have been far from the truth. The ambiguous, undisclosed nature of NM would have piqued Tae-seong's curiosity, and he probably thought that if he just kept putting himself out there, he would get his way in the end. He had likely been expecting this day to come.

Now then, all is to plan, right, Tae-seong? You think we're just going to have a bit of a lovers' tiff and then I'm going to let you win, right? Then we can be happy ever after? Let's see about that.

"This isn't how you approach a woman," I told him.

"I'm sorry?"

"Women aren't your meal tickets."

"I'm sorry, I don't understand."

"I mean, fuck off, you son of a bitch."

Tae-seong flinched for a second, but then scoffed. *Don't scoff at me, you con man!* I yelled internally. I stood up with my unfinished coffee. I was sure Tae-seong would stop approaching me now that I had seen right through him. Tossing the coffee in the trash, I left the café. He didn't fight back or follow me out, but I felt like Tae-seong's conceited scoffing was stuck to the back of my head.

I was left with a bad taste in my mouth, and I didn't know why.

Later, I took a look at the information the director had acquired from the NM intelligence team, and I realized that Tae-seong was more cunning than I thought. He had a habit of taking various hobby classes and workshops with women, which made it easy for him to get their attention and approach them under the guise of shared interests. He would then casually accompany the women to local festivals and hiking trips, being nice to them in small, subtle ways.

After the relationship had progressed, but just before it reached its peak, he would bring up some sort of financial proposition. A relationship at that stage was full of desire and raring to get to the next stage, so just when the women were utterly consumed by passion, he would make a play for their pockets. The women would then just hand over all their money and wait for him to find somewhere to settle down.

The really shameless, disgusting part was that he would then actually "return" some of the money. Tae-seong would bring back a third of the money in tears, telling the women he got scammed and that their house-to-be was taken from him. Since they now knew his sad predicament, most of the women could not bear to use all the money they had just got back for themselves, and gave him half instead. Women, so dignified and pure of heart, could never let money get in the way of love.

Barely any reports had been made about him. *Just leave those poor women alone, for fuck's sake!* I wanted to shout. How many people had he actually hurt? I was sure the real number was far bigger than the number of reports. How many women had fallen prey to him and then suffered in silence? I never wanted to spend even another second with that man.

The director, on the other hand, blamed both Tae-seong and his victims.

"They're just crazy. Why would you go and stake your pride on something so stupid?" she said.

I got where the director was coming from; these women got tricked into falling in love, and then love made them do crazy things. I didn't get it either, but I thought it was a low blow to call them crazy, when all they were was a little stupid in love. It was hard to avoid getting conned by people whose entire goal from the start was to con you. Men like Tae-seong were the ones to blame, because the others were just victims after all. The director changed the subject.

"Well, that being said, Inji, a rematch request came through from your ex-husband."

Yikes. I had asked to be taken off the dispatch list because I wanted to take some time off from being in the field and just work at the office for a while instead. I was looking forward to spending some time at home, but now here was this rematch request.

"When do I need to start?" I asked.

"As soon as possible, by the looks of it."

"I'll let you know when I'm ready."

"Don't rush into it."

"I won't."

"As you know, a rematch after a first marriage will get you good performance reviews. You've done well," the director said, giving me a gentle clap on the shoulder before returning to her seat.

It did seem weird, even to me. I didn't have much

trouble putting up with the weirdos who I met through NM, but maybe that was because they seemed like at least somewhat decent people. On the other hand, I just couldn't stand the weirdos I met outside, in my actual life. It wasn't like I was stuck here, in this world, because of them, but I still resented them. All they did was destroy things, and if they just left it alone, the world would automatically become all nice and beautiful. Those women were fine by themselves, even without any romance in their lives, so I wished Tae-seong would just leave them alone. He exhausted me.

I needed to just disappear and go do my job, quietly, away from everyone and everything. *Why do I always end up taking refuge in NM?*

6

I gave my long-neglected car a good wash and got it waxed. Whenever I was on an assignment, I would leave it parked in the office car park, so even though it was a three-year-old car, its mileage hadn't even reached ten thousand kilometers. I had a feeling that it was going to break that record during this trip, though. The car was on its best behavior, racing along at a good hundred kilometers an hour, as though it were a brand-new ride out for its first spin on the freeway. It wasn't like I was eagerly rushing toward my destination, so I didn't go out of my way to overtake anyone, and just stayed in my lane instead.

I was going to pay my mother a visit before starting my assignment. I had to report to her from time to time, in small doses, so that I could avoid being summoned too frequently. Otherwise, I was subjected to one-sided "conversations" with her. These were not, by any means, productive conversations that led to any useful conclusions. I had tried raising my voice, and even just walking away, but it was hopeless; my mother never changed.

But now, I knew how to avoid her—I would act like I understood what "wasn't right." Our ideas of what was or wasn't right were so different that we would never see eye to eye, so pretending was the only option I had. It was the only way we could maintain even some superficial semblance of a normal mother-daughter relationship.

The GPS announced that the exit was seven hundred meters ahead. I checked the odometer, surprised. When had I covered all that distance? I had just been driving onward, senselessly, as if I were asleep at the wheel. I had no recollection of driving with any alertness, and had been in this blank state for about four hours.

I felt a chill down my spine. Why was I arriving so soon to a destination I didn't want to visit? I suddenly wished that I was stuck in traffic, but the car continued to speed down the road without pause. The journey had been too easy.

As I crossed the toll gate, I immediately found myself in the city center. I could even see the grocery store my older brother worked at. The town covered a considerable area, but its population couldn't have been more than a hundred thousand people. It was a small and cozy city, one of many in the country's southern region. The traditional Korean markets and the nearby village were always bustling with activity.

My parents seemed to enjoy the place. I guess as people who had only ever lived in Seoul, they enjoyed the novel experience, finding things to snack on, or chancing upon fresh groceries to make Korean side dishes with. Whenever they wanted to get some fresh air, they packed lunchboxes and made their way to the rest stop located halfway up Jiri Mountain. They liked the fact that there was no need to hike all the way up to the summit—they could see the mountains from their house every day anyway. Their apartment was right opposite a stream. They had previously said that they were sick of apartments, but they still chose to live in one again.

My mother was sitting near the flowers and stood up when she saw my car pull into the driveway. I slowly approached.

"Here, park here," called my mother. "Have you had anything to eat?"

"Yeah. Where's Dad?"

"He'll be down soon. He's getting all dappered up to take you to the market."

I had barely arrived and I was already being whisked

away to a market. My father came down to join us, wearing a suit and a matching fedora. Not exactly my idea of a typical market outfit, but he disagreed.

"Everyone comes to the market dressed up," he insisted. "We're late. Let's go."

We drove out to the town hall. The rest of the city seemed quiet. The market itself was extremely crowded; it was like being in downtown Seoul on New Year's Eve. Judging by the procession of people at the bus stop, it seemed like the entire nation's elderly had come here. There was definitely more than a bus or two full of them.

My father went ahead, pushing through the crowd to enter the market. There was so much to see that I couldn't keep up with him. A delicious smell came from some ugly-looking doughnuts at a stall. I could see them put rolls of dough one after the other into the frying oil, and it made me want to go have a taste. I gave the old lady running the stall five thousand won for what I assumed would be a doughnut or two, but she seemed to have mistaken it for fifty thousand won and kept adding doughnuts to my plate.

"Excuse me, I only asked for five thousand won worth of doughnuts," I said.

"If you can't finish all of the doughnuts, just pop them in the microwave for thirty seconds, and they'll taste like they're fresh."

I saw seafood stalls with buckets that had more loaches than water in them. I then saw a stall selling excessive amounts of strawberries for only five thousand won. At that price, you would almost feel bad for buying them. You could probably take a bath in the juice of about ten thousand won worth. The strawberries had a nice sheen and fragrance to them.

Long ago, I had gone to some popular five-day market with Shi-jeong, and had left feeling disappointed. If anything, it had been more expensive than just going to a regular supermarket. It was so packed with souvenirs, you saw them everywhere you looked. There were also restaurants with banners touting that Mr. Such-and-Such had stopped in here, and Mrs. So-and-So had visited. The excessive marketing was annoying. There was nothing like that here, and yet, it was packed enough to contend with any of the more famous markets.

It also had that particular atmosphere of the country-side. There was that unique twang to everyone's speech. The longer you listened to people speak, the more it sounded like a traditional Korean *madangnori* performance. My mother stood in front of the side-dish store she was a regular at. The lady who owned the store looked at me.

"Yeah, she just came down from Seoul for a bit. I

wanted to send her back with a bunch of food," my mother replied.

My mother asked for perilla leaf kimchi, pickled *deodeok*, and pickled Korean melon. The owner added even more perilla kimchi to what was already packed and threw in some green onion kimchi as a freebie.

My father very excitedly took us to a *soondae gukbap* restaurant. Mountains of plump blood sausage and boiled meat adorned the entrance. The owner of the restaurant was standing at the entrance and immediately recognized my father.

"Well, now, who's this young lady? I don't think I've seen you around!"

"This is our daughter. None of the other girls hold a candle to her, do they?"

"If you saw our youngest, you'd be bowled over stunned. Don't just stand there blocking the door, come in and take a seat."

The shop was bustling with clusters of customers sitting together. The owner, whose daughter, by the way, was so beautiful she made people swoon, brought out our plates of soondae, as well as bowls of soondae stew. The sausages were filled with *seonji*, which took me by surprise, as I'd never seen soondae stuffed with blood jelly before. I added it to the piping hot soondae stew to give it a try. I ate and ate, but the meat was never-ending.

I had thought that, in the provinces, they added extra salted seafood to their kimchi, but their kimchi was not as salty as my mother's, and even their side dishes were light and fresh.

"It doesn't matter where you eat here, the food is always delicious. It's like the people here were born with their hands smothered in marinade."

My mother always said that the food in that region was the best in the country. She said the people were as nice as the cuisine, so there weren't many unpleasant fights breaking out between neighbors or anything. Who knew this tiny place was full of such hidden charm?

When we were done and about to leave, I suddenly noticed that my hands were full of shopping bags. Apparently, when I was in the market, I would think, *Oh, what's that?* And just like that, it would be in my hands. As far as I remembered, all I had done was remark that certain products were cheap, that they looked good, that the food looked delicious, but now, somehow, the trunk of my car was packed full of stuff.

My mother said that she had the same experience when she first came to the market. My father poked fun at her. "Your mom spends her money on everything she sees—soon she'll start buying men off the streets as long as they're cheap."

"Oh, the nerve of this man!" she exclaimed.

★ ★ ★

All we did was visit the market in the morning and take a short walk along the riverbank in the evening, but the day flew by and it was already night. My father packed his blankets and went into the living room, while I lay in bed with my mother. It had been a long time since I had shared a bed with her.

"You said you were going to China for work this time, right? Make sure you eat well," she said.

"There's a lot of good food in China."

And then, there was nothing else to say, as was often the case when I was with my mother.

"You know, you should really try to find your own match instead of setting up others."

"Yeah, maybe I should."

"Try to marry someone like your brother. I've never seen a man who's as diligent and handsome as your brother."

"I saw thousands like him at the market."

"Oh, the nerve of this girl—I've dedicated my whole life to you and your brother, you know? You owe me for that!"

My mother's words floated around my ears instead of entering them. She often said that she would have left my father if it weren't for me and my brother. My father would say the same. My brother and I felt like we had become their children because it was necessary; there was no other option. My mother, for the sake of her own honor, became like a fixture at home, slowly turning into stone as she waited dutifully for her husband to come back each night. And he would, only return because he couldn't find a suitable replacement.

I glanced at my mother. She looked bored to death. Whenever I looked at my father, he seemed angry. My parents seemed to increasingly become strangers to one another. But anyone else would see them as a happy couple, blessed with a son and a daughter. My brother and I weren't against my parents getting a divorce, so I couldn't understand why they continued living like that.

Granny from next door seemed happier in comparison. She was single, but completely unbothered, and she did not cling to superficial relationships. In our family, you could do nothing at all but still feel exhausted. I felt my eyes start to droop.

I dreamed that I was doing a folk dance, dancing around in a wonderfully colorful, multilayered dress, with large paper flowers in my hair. In my dream, I was spinning around, holding up the end of my dress and greeting people, before coming to a stop in front of my mother. "You went around and around, but saw nothing special, right?" she said to me. My mouth froze; I could not speak. It was such an intense dream.

★ ★ ★

The next morning, I washed up quickly, only taking the time to put on some sunscreen, then immediately wore my shoes. If I hung around too long, I would be subjected to one of my mother's elaborate breakfasts. These were usually unpleasant, awkward meals endured in silence, like we were monks eating at a temple. I did feel bad—my mother had likely woken up early to cook breakfast for her dear daughter who she would not be seeing for a while, but I saw no other option. Because I found it unpleasant to be around my mother, I felt the same about her food.

My parents came to the car to see me off. My father loaded the side dishes we had bought at the market into the trunk.

"How are you going to drive on an empty stomach? Have some *chueotang* with Dad before you leave."

"I had a lot to eat yesterday, I'm fine."

"Stop by a rest stop and eat something on the way."

"Okay."

"When you go on your trip abroad, be careful and drink clean water."

I gave my mother a slight nod and slowly pressed the accelerator. Since I had very reluctantly made this trip to my parents' house, I thought I would feel better when I left. But I still felt a heaviness in my heart.

* * *

"Everything is delicious," Granny remarked as she tasted the side dishes I had brought from my visit. I was leaving for my assignment soon, so I gave everything to Granny to enjoy.

"Looks like your mom's really living the good life with your old man, eating all this delicious food."

"It's quite nice where they are. You should visit sometime."

"I should…"

Granny had been troubled of late. Her son and his wife had shut down their business and all they were left with now was debt. Apparently, they had been quite harsh with Granny, going as far as to say that their issues did not matter to her anymore and all she cared about was the young singer oppa. But what could she do? She said it was love. I wondered if her son might have been accepting of the relationship if his business had been successful. Maybe, but even if things were different, he probably would've been unhappy about his mother's love life.

For Granny, having to look after her grandson until late every evening was an additional source of frustration. She had to bear her son's insults all day and then go take care of his child at night. Again, what else could she do? He was her only grandchild.

Despite all of this, she got her eyebrows done again.

The eyebrow tattoo from her previous micro-blading session had turned blue, so she got it lasered off and re-done. Her face was becoming scarier by the day. Her double eyelids still didn't sit right on her face, for some reason. At this rate, she could offer to buy the young oppa a new house, and he might still choose to leave her and run away.

7

To begin our remarriage, the husband and I exchanged our wedding vows, and the senior executive from NM declared us married. It felt a bit rushed. Hurrying through the ceremony, the company seemed to be saying, *No one likes a wedding that drags on too much. Let's just get it over with it and move on to the eating part.*

The senior executive put the wedding rings provided by NM on our fingers. They were gem-less, plain fourteen-karat thread rings. What set these apart from the plain band I had from my last wedding was the subtle engraved design on them. I had a feeling the two rings would look pretty great if I wore them together. The husband and I marked the end of the wedding by popping a bottle champagne given to us by NM.

Since it was a remarriage, the event was quite a simple

affair. The director was there too and, as she was leaving the house, she held my hand and stroked the ring. Her nose slightly red and stuffy, she wished me luck. "Be good," she told me. *I'll do my best*, I thought. It felt like she was sending off her own daughter.

We all hopped in a BMW and drove off, passing a green onion field on the way. Weirdly, a part of the patch looked squished, like someone had stomped on it or dug through it. I wondered where all those onions had disappeared to. The flowers on the onion plants looked so lovely, like little bouquets. For some reason, I had an empty feeling in my chest.

The husband put his arm around my shoulder, and I hooked mine around his waist.

"The groom's looking sharp today."

"I made an effort. Let's head inside."

The dress I had worn for the ceremony was simple, ornamented only by the wrinkles in its fabric. I took it off and changed into a pretty loungewear dress. It seemed like bad manners to dress casually in a plain T-shirt on the first day.

This was my first time in a remarriage contract. I was unpacking again, in the same house, with the same luggage. If I had known that I would be returning this quickly, I wouldn't have thrown away all the things I had used during our previous marriage. As I opened the dresser drawer, the husband embraced me from behind.

"I was worried you would say no."

"If I say no one more time, I will be let go. Using that no on you would be a waste."

"In that case, I should've asked for a three-year contract."

"Then I would have said no."

"Why?"

"Because I like to switch things up."

Before I could finish even taking the clothes out of my suitcase, we were passionately undressing each other. *What is with this man? Did he set this marriage up just so he could play sex addict?* I moved my body against his. It looked like he had been using his fancy soundproof studio to watch porn, because he was trying out bolder positions than he had during our previous marriage. I even got some foreplay, and he sat me on his lap. He still lacked the skill, but he was trying to make up for it with effort, and he kept switching up positions. But it was unsatisfying, like he was doing it but not *really* doing it. This "unique" sex was just not cutting it for me. Soon, he collapsed on top of me, all the wind blown out of him.

Sex with him had become a bit more exciting, there was a bit more variety, but like before, he still could not fill me up completely. Why then, did he keep asking,

You like that? Would he like it if all I did was indecisively move my tongue around, instead of sucking him off properly? I left my husband as he was—lying flat on the bed, satisfied with his new techniques—and went to the bathroom. I wondered why he was taking this marriage so seriously.

The husband still had the habit of buying booze when he got drunk, but I was used to it now. The stuff about alcohol no longer stressed me out, and I had no intention of putting any stress on the husband because of it. It was nice to have an array of stuff to choose from whenever I was in the mood for a drink and, besides, having some alcohol on hand was quite useful in the kitchen, since certain recipes called for it. While I had definitely seen people die from drinking too much alcohol, I had never seen anyone die from *buying* too much alcohol.

And yet, as nice as it was to pick out and enjoy a drink, my growing love handles were a problem. The husband didn't usually eat while drinking, but I couldn't do without munching on some snacks. The husband once remarked that I seemed to drink to eat. If this continued, I would be celebrating my thirtieth birthday with a thirty-inch waist.

I had tried exercising with hula hoops and jump ropes but my belly fat, indifferent to my plight, kept claiming more space. Since I couldn't see any noticeable results, exercise became boring. So, I started pulling out weeds in the backyard. Every day, I set out a fixed area of the yard and pulled out weeds. I was clearing them out gradually, little by little, but I had soon filled an entire paint tub with clippings to be discarded. Later, the husband brought some newspaper and a lighter to burn the grass. He lit the fire. It crackled as it burned.

"I'm going to the office tomorrow," I said.

"But I was going to go look at speakers with you. Do you have something else on?"

"The director wanted to meet. I'm going to get dinner with her."

"Guess it can't be helped."

The dinner tomorrow was for Yoo, who, in the end, couldn't keep the baby and got an abortion. She could have taken a bit more time off, but she came straight back to work. She needed comfort. If we pretended not to see her pain, she would have no one else to rely on.

The director invited me to the dinner because I had been like a mentor to Yoo at work. She had always had this naive sweetness about her, right from the start. She was adamant about wanting to reject all marriage contracts until there was one she liked, even though she knew that a series of constant rejections led to resignation. And then she got her first husband. She said yes to him because he seemed nice, and now she was even carrying his child. But she wouldn't be able to give birth to it. To think that her very first marriage would be so painful. It was just proof that things never went the way you wanted them to.

I pulled out a couple more weeds and threw them into the old paint tub.

"Honey, what was your marriage like, the one before you joined NM? Can I ask about stuff like this?" I asked the husband.

"Well, you've already asked, so I'll say you can. I felt like I had been consumed by the system."

He said that during his marriage, he constantly had that feeling you have when you blow into a breathalyzer, or suddenly step on the brakes because you see speeding cameras installed on the road. He couldn't say anything to his wife, since she never meant any harm. If he did, he ended up looking like some jerk who was just out to fight for no reason. Their arguments always followed the same pattern:

"You can't do that!"

"Yeah, I know."

"Then why are you doing it?"

"I don't know."

"Do you know why you shouldn't be doing this?"

"Yeah, I do."

"So why do you keep on doing it?"

The husband said that they used to have the same type of quibbles when they had first moved in together, but it felt different back then. Once they were married, it was like his wife had been given the legal right to bend him to her will. He said that living in that environment was overwhelming and difficult to manage.

"After you get married, every aspect of your life is open to interference, including from the state," he elaborated. "Our marriage was an agreement between the two of us, so why do the courts have to get involved? All we did to get married was hand in a form—why couldn't a divorce be that simple too? Maybe they think everyone will scramble to get a divorce if it is that easy. But there would still be people who would never get a divorce, even if the state asked them to. And it's not like the government's finding you a perfect spouse—if they really want to stop divorce, that's what they need to do."

"I guess they need to be so strict with the divorce process *because* they're not doing anything else to prevent it. Marriage sounds exhausting," I replied.

"It was for me. But why do you ask? Do you have some romantic fantasies about marriage or something?"

"Well, I don't know, maybe? There is that aspect of having someone to help. Let's say something bad happens to me—wouldn't my husband be the first to run over and help?"

"Uh, there are a lot of couples that get into fights because the husband was the last to arrive!" he joked.

The husband went on to say that his marriage felt like riding along in a caravan, driving across an endless desert. No matter how good the caravan was, the husband was thirstier and thirstier for the hazy illusion that he believed would exist in a place he considered to be an oasis. To other people, it would seem like he had enough food and fuel, but to the husband, even people with a single bottle of water riding camels were better off. To make matters worse, the caravan also kept complaining. "I'm not made to cross deserts!" it would protest. The husband said that he and his wife were exhausted for their own reasons, and there was nothing that they wanted from each other anymore, so they separated.

"Still, you ignored what everyone else was saying and managed to break up, in the end," I said.

"Talking about it now that it's all done makes it seem easy, doesn't it? In divorce, you just take a bottle of water and leave the caravan. Some people even skip the water and just grab their gaggle of kids. If the caravan is on the verge of an inevitable explosion, then you just have to run, right? You have no choice. Everyone's going to die anyway, so you might as well try and do something. But there's a chance that the caravan won't blow up, so I don't think it's right to pull out the steering wheel and puncture the tires in retaliation before going on your way. Who knows, it might drive better in the hands of another driver."

"Between you and your ex-wife, who was the caravan?" I asked.

"We both were. Driver, then caravan, perpetually switching between those two roles. That's marriage."

"Why'd you become an NM member?"

"Because I managed to escape the desert."

"I guess there's no need for an oasis anymore then?"

"You know, if it weren't for the desert, everything would be an oasis."

My husband put down the tongs and pushed me against the backyard table. I was a little surprised by his sudden eagerness on this dusky and quiet night. I was his oasis now. I would give my body to him. I'd really do anything to keep him happy. But this position wasn't too great; my stomach was too cold against the table. I wouldn't have thought my first time having outdoor sex would be this uncomfortable. My skin chafed against the rough surface of the table, so I decided it would be better to sit on the table instead. I told the husband to hold on for a moment as I pushed myself onto the table and put one leg on the chair. The husband excitedly rushed back into me once I gave him the signal to do so. Not even a minute later, he came. He seemed a bit embarrassed and laughed, still holding me.

"Let's go again later. It's so hot when you put your leg up here like that," he said.

I just smiled and pulled on the pants that were hanging onto one leg, dampened by my husband's ejaculate, which had run down my thighs. I needed to go clean up. I should have brought out a handkerchief or something. Did I need to keep some tissues in the backyard now?

I was about to tell the husband that I was going back in, when the doorbell rang. I called out to ask who it was, but the doorbell just kept ringing. The husband rushed to the door and opened it. There was someone standing there but, my view obstructed by the husband, I couldn't see their face.

"Who is it?" I asked.

There was no answer. The husband turned to look at me and only then did I see the man's face.

Om Tae-seong.

I felt dizzy. It felt as if all the blood had drained from my body. Why was this man here, and why did he have another goddamn tteok cake box with him? What was wrong with him? Was he incapable of reading other people's emotions, or did he just not give a shit? It's like he was a machine that reset every morning and showed

up with the same expression, like we were always meeting for the first time.

He greeted me like a door-to-door salesman, with
a "Hello, how are you?" There was something perfor-
mative about Tae-seong's calm and cheerful demeanor.
The husband turned to me with a look that seemed to
say, *Do you know this man?*

"He's someone I went on a blind date with once," was
my short, quick reply.

"Would you like to come in?"

The husband stepped aside. Tae-seong entered the
yard, looking around. I wanted to wrap up whatever
this was outside, but before I could say anything, the
husband led Tae-seong inside. A small thread of smoke
rose from the paint can where the fire had been burning, reminiscent of traditional mosquito repellant. Op-
pression descended upon the tranquil and idyllic scenery.
That man, he truly made it hard to breathe.

I showed Om Tae-seong to the living room and
quickly got some beers from the fridge. Since he was an
uninvited guest, I didn't bother with any snacks. I placed
the tray with the beers on the table. Tae-seong held out
the cake box toward me. *Are the rice cakes just an excuse
to get something else?* I couldn't help but wonder. As far as

unannounced invasions went, at least he had the courtesy to not arrive empty-handed.

"I made them just before coming here," he said.

"Right…thank you," I replied.

I glanced over at the cake box before putting the beer down in front of them. How was I supposed to deal with Tae-seong? How could he have known about this house? What plan was he concocting as he stalked me? Did he find out about this marriage and think that my first date with him was me cheating on my husband? Did he want hush money? It's not like I seduced him into bed. And even if I did, so what? Adultery wasn't a crime anymore. He didn't call me or try to blackmail me before this, so why had he just dropped in on us?

The husband did not say anything. He just drank his beer and observed, waiting to see how the situation would play out. I needed a way to get rid of Tae-seong. I hated this never-ending cycle I seemed to be stuck in. It felt like I was playing squash—no matter how hard I hit the ball, it would just bounce back toward me. I launched attack after attack upon the wall, but I was the one who ended up defeated. Just seeing Tae-seong drained the energy out of me.

"I suppose you have a reason for coming here?"

"Ah, the house is even nicer inside. It's got quite the floor space. You've built it yourselves, right? It'll be difficult when it comes time to sell, because of how secluded it is."

Paying no heed to my question, Tae-seong started chatting about the finishings of the house and how much of the yard was used. I left it at that. My skin crawled at his unbelievable nonchalance.

I realized then, that all this time, I had been dealing with someone who wasn't right in the head. He was the type of person who, even if you kicked him out of your life with all the strength you could muster, he would just laugh it off and show up again. He didn't even tell me off for not mentioning I was married. Though, to be fair, I didn't tell him off for following me all the way here. I cut him off as he was talking about what vegetables could be planted in the garden.

"Doesn't seem like you came over just to give us some tteok."

"Ah, no. I, uh, I came over because of that thing."

"What thing?"

"I'm not a con."

"Excuse me?"

"I've thought about this quite a bit, but it's a bit difficult to put into words. So please understand if it's a bit all over the place. Um, yes, it's true that I went to a workshop to learn how to make tteok. And yes, I also grabbed a coffee with some of the other people there, like Shi-jeong, and we talked about this and that. I think I said something like 'Why is it that every time I get set up with a "nice" girl, she turns out to be weird?' Yeah, I think that's what I said. It was a joke, but Shi-jeong took it seriously. She said that she had a friend who hated being set up with guys because she thought it was a waste of time. So, I said that it's exactly those kinds of girls—the kind that say that but end up going on blind dates anyway—that I really disliked. But we talked for a bit, and she managed to goad me into meeting up with you. That's what happened."

Okay, now I knew how I'd been set up with Tae-seong.

"I thought you were nice. I saw your smooth skin and thought you looked like a person carved from soap."

"But why did you keep showing up to see me?"

"Just because. But I never interrupted your work, did I?"

Tae-song drank the beer and laughed, even coughing a bit.

"Oh, this is just so funny. This beer is delicious, the temperature is just right. Ah, what was I talking about? Right, cons. I'm not a con. Apparently you thought that I kept turning up because I was after money. That's not it, I was just curious. I don't get why people hate me so much. Why do *you* hate me? What did I do wrong?"

Tae-seong had another sip of his beer. Now I could see why my body had reacted to him with fear. He lived completely in his own head. That was why my firm re-jection didn't deter him. It was like he was performing a one-person-play—he listened to the things he said and agreed with himself. To him, it wasn't important that I had a husband—we were just the audience, there to watch his play. Talentless and one-sided, Tae-seong rig-orously followed his own lead, oblivious to his rudeness to others. This wasn't even a fight to him. He was that much of a psychopath. I had always used that word as a joke, but this was no laughing matter.

"So, have you stopped working?" Tae-seong asked me. "Or can staff from the third floor work from home? Ah, you're not going to tell me, are you? You never do. But seriously though, I'm not a con man. Well, it's not really important, but what I'm trying to say is—why do you hate me? Why do you despise me so? What made you hate me the moment you saw me? *What* did I do? I'm not trying to blame you or anything, I'm just curious, that's all. Oh, do you want to see the rice cake? I coated it with black sesame powder, so it's nice and looks pretty."

Why did I hate him? How was I even supposed to make him understand? *I just hate your existence, Om Tae-seong. Would you accept my reason, even if I gave you a logical one?* The rules of general logic did not apply to Tae-seong. Even if he got rid of the qualities I hated about him, I still wouldn't like him. He was just awful.

I was really trying to kill time while the rescue team arrived, but I still hadn't gotten a response from them. I knew that they got delayed sometimes, but this was taking way too long. I wished they would just hurry up and drag him out of the house.

Om Tae-seong home invasion right now, I had texted the director when I went to get the beers. But still, no response.

Eventually, the rescue team arrived, only after Tae-seong had sung a few more praises of his rice cake. The director herself came, with two men accompanying her. Like a guest who was expected for dinner, she entered and said airily, "Sorry we're late."

"Hello, looks like we meet each other again," she said to Tae-seong.

The director introduced Om Tae-seong to one of the men that was with her. The man extended his hand for a handshake, and Tae-seong awkwardly extended his own as well. Instead of shaking it, the man pulled Tae-seong by the hand and twisted his arm behind his back. The other man covered Tae-seong's mouth and nose with a handkerchief. His eyes drooped shut, suggesting that the handkerchief had probably been doused with some kind of anesthetic.

I hadn't expected them to take him out like that—it

was instant. The two men did not take long to put Tae-seong into a sleeping bag and leave. It was like they were capturing a feral, stray dog.

"My apologies for arriving so late," the director said to the husband.

"It's all right," he responded.

I walked out to the front yard with the director as she was leaving.

"I'm sorry."

"It's okay. We'll take care of him. The whole thing must have been a bit of a shock for you."

"Yes."

"You responded calmly. Good job."

"What's going to happen to Tae-seong?"

"We'll look after him. Get inside. Your husband's waiting."

The world was so unbelievably violent. I didn't dare express my own opinions. I just had to put on a smile, as if nothing happened. This was the world of NM.

I got straight to tidying up the table, clearing away the beer and tteok cake. There couldn't be any traces of another man in the house. The husband took the tray I was holding and put it back on the table.

"You could've given that man a chance."

"Let's not poke our noses into each other's business."

I wasn't sure when the husband had become so aroused, but the next thing I knew, he was pushing his hardened cock inside me, keeping the promise he had made in the front yard.

A man had just been taken away by an ambulance with no sirens. He would be detained in a hospital as a person with no family. He might even be declared a patient with a serious illness. *Oh, this is going to be really frustrating for you, Mr. Om Tae-seong. NM has no leniency.* The company didn't like it when people created trouble. Tae-seong may come out of it all, but probably only after losing a few marbles. And if he decided to open his mouth, NM would get straight to making sure no one believed him.

"You like that?" the husband asked.

"Yeah," I responded.

Did Tae-seong really have to keep seeking me out even though I had rejected him early on? NM wasn't structured the way it was for the sake of its employees. Its services were designed purely for its clients, and they were meticulous in dealing with anything that would disturb a client's peace. The husband was really feeling it today.

"You like that?"

"Yeah."

8

My body felt so heavy and drained that I couldn't imagine leaving the house, but I knew I needed to go to work, if only to file a report about yesterday's altercation. I was itching for a good drink with people I could be completely honest with. At the office, I filed the report, and I must have written about a million apologies in it. "I apologize; this was a grave error; I am absolutely at fault; please excuse my behavior; I sincerely regret…" and on and on. With every line I wrote, my thirst for a drink only grew. *I'm so fucking sick of this, why is my life such shit?*

The director sensed my mood and discreetly slipped away with Yoo and me, without our other colleagues noticing.

"How'd you get so thin overnight? You look like death," the director asked.

"I committed the sin of going on a blind date, so I had to really put my body to work to earn my forgiveness."

"Then we need to replenish your energy levels. Let's drink!"

We clinked soju glasses and downed the contents.

"How are you doing? How are you feeling?" I asked Yoo.

Yoo laughed quietly at my questions. At NM, love was temporary. We could never forget that we were FWs. For us, love was only permitted within the constraints of a contract and a fixed term. Accidents happened when you mistakenly assumed that you were somehow special. To our clients, we were all the same.

"I've never met a man who hates children that much."

Or maybe clients just hate the children that pass through our bodies, I thought to myself. I was glad that Yoo's husband had said it that way. It was the least he could do for her. I hoped that Yoo would just accept his reason at face value, and not think too deeply about the real, honest truth about her situation. That would be too painful. When you realized that yours was a body that wasn't permitted to give birth, you couldn't bring yourself to love it, even though it was your own.

Maybe things might have been different for her with a different husband. Even in our profession, we were rarely having babies with the men we slept with. Not all sex was about having children. "All life is precious and must be protected." Only good people with good hearts respected that kind of rule. You couldn't expect much from others; they brought only useless congratulatory flowers and unwanted advice about childbirth.

I didn't blame Yoo for choosing not to have the baby in the end. I, for one, was definitely not the kind of person who would criticize her for "taking away a life." I saw Yoo's tears. I could only imagine how sad she must have been.

"I was really shaken but, as people say, I'll try and make an opportunity out of it," she said.

Was she trying to comfort herself or delude herself? I couldn't tell. In my experience, a crisis was a crisis. It was extremely unlikely for a crisis to become an opportunity. What actually happened was that you got trapped in the crisis, which clouded your judgment and made it impossible to predict that pain that your flawed decisions were going to create.

When I was offered a job at NM by that scout, my acceptance was neither an escape nor an opportunity. It was a decision motivated by crises. The husband's marriage was not the only place that was a desert. To me, the entire world was a desert—a desert so arid that surviving it was a feat. The desert was scarily apathetic to the thirst people felt. As I trudged through sandy plains, I was desperate for a sip of water, but the desert dried even the saliva in my mouth. When I bowed my head in surrender, the desert tried to break my neck for good measure. But, when I held my head high with resilience, the desert tried to chop it off with a sharpened axe. I couldn't tell what the desert wanted from me, but I suspected it was obedience. What I wanted was to just be able to walk wherever I wanted, as far as I wanted, even if my feet stared to sink into the sand.

NM was a desert that hid its falsehood, while the world outside was a desert that was wrapped entirely in falsehood. When I was little, I believed that the world would understand me once I became a grown-up. But when I became a grown-up, I realized that it was I who now understood the world. I think I got why Yoo rushed back to work at NM. The world outside NM never welcomed us with open arms. The soju burned as it went down my throat.

To lighten the mood, the director started to talk about a client currently in contract with a FW. The same client had been my third husband. He was a novelist and a serious man to larger society, but a complete laughingstock within NM. Recently, he and his young wife had been caught being naughty on a late-night bus and ended up at a police station because of it. The driver saw them in the rearview mirror and, concerned that something strange was happening on his bus, stopped in front of a police station. He must have been pretty shocked to see an elderly man passionately kissing a woman young enough to be his granddaughter.

The wife immediately contacted the director, who, fortunately, lived nearby. The director rushed over and immediately smoothed things over, saving the author from a scandal in the papers. When the director reprimanded the novelist, he said that he had always wanted to have a passionate kiss on the bus. *Oh, this man, he's truly something*, I thought. I asked the director how she handled the situation. She told us that she explained to the police that the young woman was actually his wife, and it ended with just a verbal warning. The author wasn't too famous; most people hadn't even heard of him.

"It must be hard for him—he really woke up to his desires quite late in life," the director commented. "What was he like, Inji? I remember reading the report. I don't think there were any big problems, were there?"

"He was all right," I responded.

The truth was that I fought more with that old man than I had with any of my other husbands. I felt like I had used up a lifetime's worth of curses on him. Glory be to the person who invented the word *fuck*. Still, I didn't pack up and end the marriage, because he had occasional endearing moments. Being a bachelor with little dating experience, he had a lot of pent-up sexual desire that he was finally getting to expend. It was like he couldn't bear to die without getting it all out of his system; that would feel unfair. At one point, he hurt my nipples so much that I had to put ointment on them. I showed him the ointment and told him not to touch my breasts for a while. Then he asked quietly, "Babies can breastfeed even after you've applied ointment, right? So, I guess it's safe to eat."

"Come again?"

"Never mind."

Once, he wanted me to bury my face in his crotch when he was writing.

"I'm going, the company can punish me for it, I don't give a fuck anymore!" I yelled at him. "Mr. Writer, are you under the impression that I'm here to be your sex slave? You're disgusting, honestly. Why are you acting like some kid who's just had his first wet dream? Would it kill you to keep your hands to yourself? Cut it out, please!"

"I'm still young at heart."

"Well, then find a way to get off telepathically."

The writer didn't have too much experience, but he was full of all kinds of desires and fantasies. Sex in the bath is entirely different to sex in the bed. The water pressure makes thrusting nearly impossible, so you need to be completely pressed against each other and move slowly. I don't know what kind of wild movies he was inspired by, but he couldn't even get inside me properly and all he did was turn the bathroom into an ocean by splashing so much water around. Even a professional swimmer would break a hip trying to thrust in the water like that. It didn't work. He got out of the bathtub and left. I had been simply enjoying a bath when he came in and made such a mess of things.

One day I asked him upfront, "What are you in such a rush for?"

"I plan on being cremated when I die. It will be so embarrassing for me if there are *sarira* crystals in the ashes."

Sarira crystals were usually found in the ashes of "pure" Buddhist monks who had managed to evade sexual temptation their whole lives. For monks, it was a sign of spiritual enlightenment, but for the writer it would be a source of shame.

In his youth, he had been terrified of ruining his reputation, and as his reputation increased, his goal was to find a woman who would solidify his fame. But his standards went higher than his actual position in society, and the constant worrying about his reputation led to a pretty lonely life.

To him, being in a relationship with a mediocre woman would be as embarrassing as having *sarira* in his cremated remains. He wanted the kind of woman that other people would look at and say, "Of course the fine author chose such a fine wife!" For a woman like that, the writer would become the type of husband who brought his wife breakfast in bed. However, those kinds of women all married other men. The only women he was left with were capable of making him big, elaborate feasts with ten different dishes, but they still could not meet his high standards.

As time went on, he would have accepted women who could only give him small, dull dinners, but even they began disappearing. People started to regard him with suspicion, wondering why he was still unmarried. As more time passed, even being a divorcé seemed better than being unmarried. People were starting to think that no one *wanted* to marry him, that there was something wrong with him.

A survey NM once conducted revealed that there was, in general, a greater preference for divorced men over men who had never married. The most common primary reason cited was that unmarried men were more likely to be self-centered. Other, additional reasons included the opinion that they had less sex appeal. When we saw these results, we joked that the lack of sex appeal, while put under the Additional category, was probably the main reason unmarried men were unpopular.

A survey about unmarried women versus divorced women was also conducted and showed similar results. However, compared to unmarried men, unmarried

women were treated with far more mockery and ridi-
cule in the responses. They were perceived as women
who *could not* get married, not as women who *did not*
get married. Even other women were quite horrible to
them. Many unmarried women reported meeting other
women who wore their marriage like a badge of honor,
and would say, "You're not married?" as an insult more
than a question. Divorcées reported similar experiences.
They would meet women who felt a sense of superi-
ority for keeping their marriages going. And then, of
course, came the final nail in the coffin, hammered in
by married women after all their other taunts. "Did I
say anything wrong?" *No, no, you just seemed a little de-
ranged, that's all.*

So, the general opinion seemed to be that getting married and then regretting it later was better than never
getting married at all.

After my contract with the old writer ended, I received a slew of marriage requests from men his age. Exhausted by my previous marriage, I said no to the next
couple. No matter how much extra pay I would get for
older clients, I didn't think I could get through another
relationship like that.

I wondered what that ex-husband thought of NM.
When I was writing my postmarriage report, I kept
writing and deleting and rewriting, just like he did when

he wrote his books. He had not been a great spouse, but I couldn't say anything too negative about him. I kept thinking about one time when he said, quietly, as though to himself, "I just couldn't use up all the love I have inside me…"

Based on what we were hearing from the director, it seemed like the old writer was just getting worse. He was apparently popping pills; it was like he was determined to keep at it until his dick wore out and fell off. This wasn't born out of some inherent loneliness of an artistic soul or anything like that. This was the result of a lifetime spent suppressing his desires, until so much of it had built up inside of him that it all came bursting out.

It wasn't like he had never dated. He had once fancied a woman and dated her for a bit, but then started to think that he was too good for her. He would look down on her in subtle ways, with all the authority of a distinguished writer. And so, she got sick of it and left. He had never had sex with her.

Apparently, he'd also had a prior, more loving relationship, one that happened only because he was a writer. In any case, I heard that the woman soon started to have complaints: "All he's good at is writing, he doesn't have much else to offer." But still, the writer often spent the night with her. Then suddenly, one day, taking his clothes off in front of her felt ridiculous. Soon after, the woman also started to feel like taking her clothes off in front of him was ridiculous. So, she wished him luck, and went on her way.

If the writer died now, I didn't think *sarira* crystals would be a concern for him anymore, but he should probably worry about what the undertaker would say when they saw that his penis was so worn-out it was practically gone. I didn't know how much writers earned. At one point, he was a big enough author that his name on the cover was enough to sell books so, unless he had wasted his wealth on something stupid, he probably had a fair amount of it. But if he kept paying for all the marriage contracts, he was bound to soon go broke. It was an addiction.

When I was with him, I used to wonder how he could keep living like that. Mr. Dignified Classy Author was going to end up in some shabby hovel at this rate. There had been members who lived pretty okay, middle-class lives, only to eventually fall behind on membership payments, and get kicked out of NM. They kept reaching out to NM, unable to let go, but our response was simple: "Get a real, legal marriage; it's the cheapest option." And we never forgot to give them some additional precious advice: "If you play your cards right, you'll have what you need, for free, for the rest of your life! But make sure your marriage is properly registered. That way, when you have complaints, you'll have the legal right to shout about them, and you might even make some good money if you decide to end things. We can talk again then."

Judging by the way he was acting, it seemed like the end was near for the old man.

The director clicked her tongue in annoyance, as if she had been the writer's lover in some distant past. "What a disgustingly sexy life, and at his old age," she remarked.

"He doesn't have too much longer left. His remaining time is precious. That's why he can't resist when he sees a pretty, tender woman—because he doesn't know if he'll ever have a woman again," I responded. "It's not about the eye candy, it's about having someone to touch. Don't include the really young girls on his list. They lose their nerve and can't even fight back like I can. It'll only cause them shame and hurt."

"I'll keep that in mind. By the way—" the director turned to Yoo "—I can make excuses for the pregnancy, tell them it happened because you're new, and haven't had too much experience, but this kind of contract-breaking leads to serious disciplinary action, so you'll have to prepare yourself for a pay cut."

"Okay. But can you please put me on the dispatch list quickly?"

"Why? You can work in the office for now, catch a break from fieldwork."

"I don't have anywhere to live."

She doesn't have a house to live in... I couldn't look Yoo in the eyes and circled my forefinger around the rim of my soju glass. There were barely any field wives who took this job for financial reasons. Our recruiters were careful to filter out those who showed visible signs of destitution and hunger on their face. Most of the women who joined in search of real prostitution work terminated their marriage contract early. For sure, FWs earned more than your average employee, but they could not compete with the women in the upper echelons of the adult entertainment industry. And you didn't get a taste of your earnings straight away either. You had to wait for your wages to be processed into your account each month.

Even then, you couldn't just spend the money whenever you wanted. If you were on an assignment, you lived with your husband, so you weren't really buying things for yourself unless you were between contracts.

Anyway, everyone had their own backstories. I never really felt the need to probe into them. People had their reasons. It was just a job after all; it wasn't like you needed some grand sense of purpose to do it. That was just rubbish you included in your cover letter when you applied. There were no such things as holy or vulgar reasons when it came to this job. You didn't get paid more for it. It was one of the things I liked about Yoo. Her life had been full of ups and downs, but she was the type of person to say, *Well, there's no need to bring all that up now*, and just laugh it off.

Yoo didn't know the exact whereabouts of her birth parents, who had only been intermittent, passing presences throughout her life. She had such a miserable and sorrowful air about her, even a landlord might feel guilty at the thought of evicting her. Despite all her suffering, she never passed on her pain to other people.

"I just always managed to find somewhere to stay," she told us.

In high school, Yoo lived in the partitioned kitchen corner of a daycare. A small foldable camp bed was her desk, her wardrobe, and her home. She helped with the cleaning and got food in return from the lunch lady. Sometimes she played with the children who stayed behind when their parents were late. Yoo would wash the little aprons, blankets, and towels, then climb up the dark staircase to go hang the laundry on the rooftop. Whenever it rained, she would have to go and retrieve the laundry, even if it was the middle of the night. After high school, Yoo helped with lessons for the daycare. She was also in charge of odd jobs here and there, like carrying the teachers' bags on field trips, or taking the children to the toilet.

Then one day, Yoo looked around and found herself sitting in a small pottery workshop. With the small earnings she had received from the owner of the daycare, Yoo moved into a windowless room in a small boarding house for students. It was a typical, cheap *gosiwon* room—tiny, and with plywood walls so thin that you could hear your neighbors yawning. But Yoo was happy because she had never had a room all to herself. Life as a workshop trainee wasn't too bad. If she arrived a little early to the workshop to get the materials ready, and stayed back a little to tidy up, her wages were enough to pay for her room at the gosiwon.

Once she started selling her own pieces, she was thinking of finally being able to move to a place with windows, when suddenly, her father appeared. He wanted money, so Yoo gave him everything she had. But apparently that wasn't enough for him. He gave her his number, asking her to get in touch when she had more money, and then promptly disappeared again. Yoo called him when she joined NM, and handed over the bank account connected to her employment to him. When the director asked her why she had done that, Yoo replied that she thought that was what she was meant to do.

"So, did your father save all that money then?" the director asked.

"I don't know. He changed his number so I can't contact him."

"Make another bank account. He doesn't have any right to spend that money."

"It won't matter if I get married, right? I'll have a house then too."

On returning to the gosiwon, Yoo felt the need for a proper place to live. She wanted to live peacefully, in a house where she could look out the windows. I remember her once telling me that she was fine with any spouse, as long as he was "capable enough," and I supposed this was her criteria. If that was the case, she had likely almost never said no to a client. The director tapped out a steady beat on the table with her nails.

"So, you really don't know where that bastard is now?"

"I don't."

"How can you not know?"

"That's just how it's always been…"

The director reached into her purse and pulled out a card, setting it in front of Yoo.

"I'll cover it myself, so just move into a room with a window and a bathroom for now."

It was so moving, but I could not cry. How could I possibly shed tears when Yoo was smiling?

"Thank you so much. I'll pay you back soon."

"I didn't ask you to pay me back," replied the director.

"Set up a new savings account as soon as you can, and I'll put your monthly salary and anything else you earn into it. If your father calls you about the decrease in your wage, put him through to me and I'll tell him there have been pay cuts because the company's going through a rough patch."

"All right."

"Hey, and here I was under the impression you were the precious youngest daughter of some wealthy family," the director joked.

We all laughed, Yoo, me, the director—but we all knew that it was superficial, that we each had things deep inside that we weren't able to say. There was a heaviness to her situation that couldn't be lifted by just some good old-fashioned cheer. Nor was her baggage something that could be shared with others once unpacked. How could I carry anyone else's baggage when I was weighed down with my own? *Your burden is as heavy as mine. I can only empathize with you.*

The director proposed a toast to my and Yoo's happiness before I could ask her any of the questions I had been mulling over. *That man, is he well? Why did you give me the wrong information? He doesn't seem like a con man, so why did you say he was?* The director was our protector, our guiding light, our fairy godmother, so surely, she probably had her reasons, right?

"Cheers," we all said and clinked our glasses together.

★ ★ ★

I took a taxi and headed home. Looking out the window, the world outside the car felt so far away, like a
world I was no longer suited to. It had been like this ever
since I fled to NM with my own two feet to escape my
mother. No matter how much I ran, I could never get
away from her. Even fathers who molested their young
daughters and mothers who burned their children with
a hot iron spent just a few years in prison then got back
into their children's lives. So how could I possibly get
away from my mother when her only crime was to stop
me from being with someone?

I still couldn't understand how someone who was so
beautiful to me could have been so disgusting to her. I
didn't know if I still loved him, but I did feel the need
to apologize to him on behalf of my mother. *I am truly
sorry.* It's not like I was completely unable to understand
my mother. She was raised that way; it was all she knew.
She couldn't accept a love that didn't conform to or re-
semble the type of love that was familiar to her. NM
was definitely a strange choice but, at the time, it was
the only place I could run to get away from her.

He's neither this nor that—he's just sickening.

I just hoped that she never said those words to him.

9

The grass had already turned yellow, since the first frost came earlier than usual this year. There wasn't a single well-shaped tree in the wide yard of the house, making it feel bleak and empty. Even if it snowed, there were no trees to be covered in snow. The lone cherry blossom tree standing next to the front gate seemed like a half-hearted gift from some Cherry Blossom Association. The yard was nice to look at when the grass was green but now, it looked dead. The husband had no interest in decorating or sprucing things up.

The day before, I had visited a specialty lighting store and purchased multiple packs of fairy lights. I thought I would decorate the withered cherry blossom tree with the lights to make it look like it was in bloom. I wound the wires along the branches. I was worried the husband would scold me for picking up an activity that took so much effort, but to my surprise, he put on his gardening gloves and came out to help.

The husband skillfully used cable ties to secure the bulbs to the tree, a job that, without his help, would have taken me several days to finish. We had to use a long extension cord to connect the lights to the outlet in the garage and it was a bit of an eyesore, but it wasn't too bad. Even just decorating the cherry blossom tree made the yard look warmer than before. There was over a month until Christmas, but it was still nice to see a tree with all its decorations up.

The house felt too frigid to me. The exterior was all gray concrete, and the interior was covered in marble. The space felt chilly even though there was heating, perhaps because it had such high ceilings. Even the pine blinds covering the windows seemed cold, with their sharp, angular lines. Maybe hanging a cosmos flower painting on the wall would help.

The husband was going to meet his friends tonight. He must have thought that they would be drinking till late, since he left his car at home. The house was quiet. It wasn't the little house in the mountains I had dreamed of, but the solitude was close to what I wanted. So then why didn't it feel like home to me? It didn't have the kind of warmth that embraced all people who came inside. It seemed tailor-made just for the husband.

I sent him a quick text.

I'm going to my apartment. I'll be spending the night. I'm taking your car.

His reply came soon after.

You know how to turn the heating on for the steering wheel, right? Stay warm, it's cold out there today.

I briefly smiled at the husband's affectionate message. He had an unexpected tenderness about him.

I received a visitor's pass from the security office and attached it to the car's windscreen. It felt weird to receive a visitor's pass to go to my own house but, nonetheless, I was happy to be there. Truly, there is no place like home.

I pressed the button to turn on the coffee dispenser. Even if I hated it, when I looked at the button, my hand automatically reached for it. Not a speck of dust had accumulated on the coffee nozzle. Granny must have diligently been taking care of it. And yet, when I would tell her to just take the machine, she wouldn't.

I had told Granny the passcode to enter the house

before I left, so that she could come in and get a coffee whenever she wanted. She had been collecting my mail while I was gone and had left it in a pile on the dining table. Most of it consisted of mail-order catalogs, with part of my address on display. What about the risk it created? Couldn't criminals find out where you lived by looking at your mail? It was a miracle that nothing bad happened the whole time I lived in the apartment. God had clearly chosen to bless this place. I tore off the parts of the envelopes that had my name and address on them and threw them all in the trash. And then the grace of God brought in Granny.

"I saw the light on and it caught me by surprise. You're back already?" she asked.

"Something came up at the office, so I came back for a bit. I have to leave again tomorrow."

I poured her a cup of coffee from the dispenser. She slurped it up, as though she were drinking soup straight from the bowl. I genuinely wanted to wrap a big ribbon around the coffee dispenser and give it to her as a gift.

After a few sips of her coffee, she gave me some sudden news.

"We're moving out of Seoul, to Pangyo."

Granny had decided, in the end, to share a house with her son and his family. Because of her son's debt, she had to put her current house up for rent in order to afford a house for them all. She would not be able to return to this house until she had saved up enough to give the tenants back their deposit.

Despite all of this, she still felt sorry for her son. He became a parent at such a young age and had to give up a lot of things most people his age enjoyed. Having a child was an event that was supposed to naturally take place at some point in the journey of a relationship. But instead, his child was a final conclusion that came right at the starting point, and changed his life into one that was completely oriented toward his son. Trying to put the child aside to live a different life was pretty much impossible. Unable to make any changes, Granny's son was stuck, forced to continue his life the way it was. The only outcome of this was increasing debt. Parents feed their children, even if it means having to beg for food. But living like beggars, surviving by accruing more and more debt, the son and his family risked being crushed by it. Granny said she felt guilty that she wasn't wealthy enough to give them a comfortable life.

"But how long do we as parents have to carry guilt for our children?" she contemplated.

"It's time your child showed you some gratitude," I replied.

"Everyone in our family, whether child or adult, seems like an infant."

"You won't be able to meet that young oppa anymore, now that you're moving away."

"I could move to a huge country like China and still find ways to meet him. Coming to the city from a little way away in the countryside is nothing for this granny."

At this point, I could not help but admire her resilience.

Granny had bought all kinds of products because of the young oppa, with the belief that she would one day use them, and in the process had turned her house into a warehouse for anything and everything. Though most of it would end up discarded, she continued blindly purchasing things. Consumerism was Granny's religion. Day by day, the things that the possessive oppa peddled kept piling up. The young oppa took advantage of Granny's desire for him, giving her both fantasies and excuses at the same time.

After all, why would a handsome young man spend his time serenading an old woman? If Granny had extra money to spend, she should just buy tickets to a performance she could actually enjoy—one where she wouldn't get ripped off. Granny was having a steamy affair all in her head, and she really needed an outlet for her pent-up desire. Her daily walks were not enough to expel all that energy.

Where was the government when you needed it? People lived to be over a hundred these days; this was an issue for an entire section of the population. Wasn't it about time there was a sexual-frustration treatment center for the single elderly? If funding was an issue, the government could look to those so-called energy drink businesses and other little side hustles that were essentially just middle-aged men and women doing sex work under the guise of door-to-door sales. If they lightened the restrictions on these businesses, it could help revitalize senior citizen libidos. As things stood, there was no sex for the elderly, and that was clearly a problem.

"Maybe I should go check out this young oppa myself," I said, teasing.

"No, you're too young. They won't let you in," Granny promptly replied, as if it were some exclusive club just for the elderly.

Granny had to put her own home that she owned up for rent in order to cover her son's debts. As someone who spent thousands on ginseng that only cost hundreds, she was not exempt from the consequences of extravagant spending. Granny got the other neighborhood grannies involved too. It was like the young oppa operated an MLM targeting the elderly. Her money, which she was supposed to use sparingly in order to have it last until she died, had all been gifted to the young oppa. She spent her money like there was no tomorrow. Granny was soon going to regret her spending habits, once she realized that people didn't die that easily. Why were the emptiest pockets the easiest to open?

Despite everything, Granny didn't criticize the young oppa. Instead, she praised him for getting her a deal that would get her a "free trip" to somewhere in Southeast Asia. If he even had a shred of conscience, he would think about how much he had pigged out on her dime, and just keep his mouth shut.

"We won't be seeing each other as much in the future. Since we're here now, should we go over to my place and have a drink?" suggested Granny.

"That sounds good."

Granny took out the *maeshil-ju* plum wine that she had made herself. There was also a yellow container of ginseng wine, which she had made for the young oppa, on the shelf. Granny had kept the fake ginseng she bought from him for herself, and then bought real ginseng at a local agricultural store to make ginseng wine for him. She seemed to have accumulated even more stuff since my last visit to her place. There were two sets of vacuums and mops, all from different makers. She also had all kinds of juice—blueberry, cranberry, raspberry, pear, grape… There was no way she was going to drink all that. Piles of unsold items from her son's business sat

alongside the piles of items that Granny had bought from
the young oppa. The thing keeping their family together
seemed to be storage efficiency.

I drank the maeshil-ju that Granny poured for me.
It was sweet.

"Aren't you seeing the young oppa a little too often?"
I asked.

"It's not like I'm tied down to an old man like your
mom. Why can't I be free and enjoy myself? Do you
think your mom could go see a handsome young oppa
if she wanted to? Even if she did, she'd probably only
do it once or twice. I hear some husbands come looking for their wives and drag them home by the ear. But
it's probably because they have such husbands that those
ladies come to see the nice oppas."

"I assume Grandpa died quite some time ago then?"

"He's not dead. He's alive and well."

Legally, Granny was still unmarried. She and Grandpa
met when they were young, falling head over heels
for one another. They lived together briefly, but then
Grandpa decided to go back to his actual wife. The only
token of love Granny was left with was her son. Mostly
absent from Granny's life, Grandpa suddenly showed up
one day and gifted her the apartment, before promptly
disappearing again. Granny had never been able to sell
it, and had only rented it out because she thought the

apartment was a father's gift for his son's future. When I remarked that she should have tried to grab ahold of Grandpa, even if it was maybe too late, she shook her head. Granny said that she was glad he had showed up, even if it was too late—he had not forgotten them and had come to help, and that was enough.

She also mentioned that she still felt apologetic toward his wife. I wondered what kind of man Grandpa must have been, for someone as proud as Granny to have willingly become his secret mistress. At the very least, he wasn't the type of man to just brush off a woman he had spent time living with. For some reason, I felt like he was probably a romantic. While the excessive cosmetic surgery had made Granny look like a botched Real Housewife of Gangnam, her pictures from back in the day showed her to be an astonishingly pretty young woman. The fact that Grandpa had been persuaded to leave such a woman to go back to his wife also made me wonder how incredible his wife must be. Granny, however, insisted that Grandpa was the most handsome one in the family.

"Can't you tell from looking at my son?" she said. "He takes after his dad, which is why he's got such killer looks."

That was just the blind love of a mother for her child. I thought of the old Korean tale of Shimcheong, who threw herself into the sea to help her blind father regain his eyesight. Granny's blindness was so incurable, a hundred sacrifices wouldn't make a difference. When I first saw her son, I was disappointed by how ordinary-looking he was, and now I knew that his father was to blame.

You hear of such good-looking boys next door that even dressed down in sweatpants they make your heart race, but where on earth could you find them? When I looked at people like my brother, who looked like a dehydrated monkfish, or Granny's son, who resembled a hungry toad, I wished we could just not have people look like that. I couldn't understand why Granny wasn't angrier at Grandpa. Maybe you needed to first cure yourself of lovesick blindness and open your eyes to be able to see someone for the toad they were.

Well go then, good riddance, Grandma should have told Grandpa. *This isn't how a person should act. Go away and take that guilt-ridden heart of yours back to your wife. Goodbye.* I wondered why the wife had never come looking for Granny. Getting a divorce would bring shame to the family, so maybe that was why she let it go. Maybe she thought, *Fine, whatever, just live with him then.* Grandpa's wife lived like that for two years, then the toad suddenly decided to hop back home. It was always the lawful wife who suffered the most in all of this.

"I didn't really take care of him that well, but my son

ended up going to a good university, and that worried me," Granny told me.

"Why?"

"His father's first son was with his wife. I heard that son kept having to retake the college entrance exam. They may have different mothers, but my son and him are still family. Would it do for the younger brother to outshine the elder?"

"That's not right. Your son hasn't done anything wrong."

"It is the original sin, the sins of the mother passed onto the son. His parents sinned, and he cannot escape it. Giving birth did not magically make my sins disappear. I'll just be glad if my grandson can avoid inheriting the consequences of my actions. The world is changing but things like this always make life more difficult."

"Hey now, your son lives by his own merits."

"Oh dear! You still like my son, don't you?" Granny teased.

You're kidding me—she's still going on about that? I could not think of a suitable reply, so I took a sip of my drink instead.

"I'll look the other way—why not give it another go?" she continued.

"Excuse me?"

"It was a joke," she said, brushing it off. "It's a shame,

but what can you do? He found his partner and he's going to spend his life with her—so forget that fool and go find someone else. Woman or man, as you get older, being single is a definite no-go. I'm telling you, you really shouldn't be alone right now. At your age, you experience a singular type of love. As you get older, the type of love you experience changes and becomes an old person's type of love. You young kids are still pretty even if you roll around in dung, so take advantage of that and love a lot!"

Maybe I needed to tell her about the owner of the car with the visitor pass, tell her he was my boyfriend or something to get her to stop going on about my dating life.

"Take the coffee dispenser with you tomorrow—" I make another attempt "—as a gift from me."

"I only use it because it's fun to come over to your place and use. Where's the fun in having it at home?"

"There isn't perhaps a coffee dispenser in the area the young oppa works, is there?"

"There is too! It's only a couple of cents a cup. But the coffee isn't even a factor. I just enjoy the attention from that pretty young thing."

Granny had fallen into a truly large bucket of shit. It had made her ill and now she was incapable of seeing anything else. If this continued, she wouldn't just reach the bottom of the bucket; she would hit the ground and her body would be buried inside the crater the impact created. She was at a place where she could not be convinced to walk away.

"Granny, I'm only asking this because I'm genuinely curious," I said sincerely, "but have you and the young oppa ever…?"

"Yeah, we've slept together," she replied. "It's a given, with the amount of money I've spent on him."

I was glad. I didn't know why, but I was relieved.

"You've done it too, right?" she asked me.

"Yeah, well, kinda, yes."

"Sex is fine, but don't get too emotionally involved. If you feel like it's not right, cut it off immediately. If it drags on, you'll be the one suffering. Be careful, because there are guys who act like husbands after just one night. Don't be too sympathetic—that's not your responsibility. You shouldn't offer up your body to someone just because you pity them. Do you understand?"

Suddenly, I felt tears run down my face.

"Money and love are the same. Have too much or too little and you lose your damn mind. You think dating a hundred people gives you a sense of security, but it feels hollow compared to a deep connection with even one person. Don't sleep around too much—date people but love deeply and for a long time. Constantly moving from one guy to the other won't help you find better men. Having too many colors in a painting makes it blurry—a single color is clear and distinct. Do you understand? I don't know why I feel so uneasy and worried when I see you."

Granny had a little more to drink, and I cried a little more.

"But, if one color drives you crazy, get rid of it quickly. Got it?" she added.

I laughed. This was why I liked Granny. That day, she gave me a surveillance mission. It didn't matter who moved in next door; if I heard them hammering nails into the wall, she wanted me to make a note of them. Granny said that if someone hammered nails into the wall without care, just because it wasn't their own house, she wouldn't renew the lease. Granny believed that too many nails in a house blocked its energy. People who rented a house could simply live in it as long as their lease lasted, but landlords had to carry the bad energy with them constantly. That was what worried Granny.

"Eventually, people die in such houses," she said solemnly.

"Oh, come on. That's not true."

"People remove the nails from the walls of the house if a person falls ill or falls on hard times—this is an age-old practice. People pull out old, rusted nails to replace them with new ones, even if the nails are set deep in the wall. Even well-embedded nails rust over time, so people pull them out and replace them with new ones."

Nobody could live in a house without hammering a single nail into it. But if any of the tenants were hammering nails to the point where the sound had become an annoyingly frequent one, then I was to tell Granny. I would be happy to do things like receive mail on her behalf or get rid of unwanted flyers, but how was I supposed to keep a check on nail-hammering? I could imagine the conversations I would have: "Excuse me, you can't hammer any nails into the wall."

"Why not?"

"It's bad luck, someone might die." Granny gave me this awkward mission, and left. She hadn't sold the house, so I was sure I'd see her again someday, but I felt emptier and sadder than I had when my own family moved out of Seoul.

10

The husband had organized a Christmas Eve party. He put a lot of effort into chopping up all the ingredients to make rice paper rolls, and prepping a tomato-and-bocconcini salad. The only thing I was allowed to do was dip the rice paper sheets in water. The husband often cooked, but today, he was really going the extra mile. It was like he had suddenly become obsessed with vegetables. I tried to make a stir-fry to add some meat to the meal, but he shut me down.

"Someone else is bringing the mains. Just prep stuff for the table."

"Did you invite someone?"

"Oh, I didn't tell you, did I? They're here already."

The husband drew open the wooden blinds. Outside, the cherry tree was all lit up. The tree had looked fine until now, but it suddenly looked like a skeleton, the light bulbs few and far between. With the bulbs spread out so much, the tree looked quite bare. Even the neon signs at the local fried chicken shop probably looked more elaborate. Now that I knew we had guests, suddenly everything looked a little shabby. Oh well, it was unavoidable. Inviting someone over meant showing them your life, the way it was. I didn't want to look too dressed up, so I wore a white cardigan over a pale purple dress.

Soon, the doorbell rang, and I heard the husband go to the door. I hurriedly powdered my face and went out to the yard.

This was this first time the husband was introducing me to one of his friends, so when I went out and saw Kim, I was a more than a little shocked.

FH Deputy Manager Kim and his spouse were our guests. Judging by the picnic basket they had brought along, this wasn't a last-minute invite. Kim's wife looked a few years older than him. Her polished bob complemented her clear complexion. She was making no attempt to hide her age, and she wore it well. She was pretty, like a sophisticated younger aunt. She had her coat on her arm, and was rolling up her khaki scarf. I had never met her before, but she walked into the house so casually it was like she had been here a million times. She introduced herself to me.

"Hi, I'm Jeong Seo-yeon."

"Welcome, please come in. I'm Noh Inji."

The husband and Kim already seemed to be acquainted. All of this seemed to be a surprise only to me, which made me feel a little uncomfortable. There were no rules against NM couples interacting, but I was a bit resentful about being the last to find out about this dinner. Kim and I gave each other a quick nod in greeting. The awkwardness of the situation aside, he was my guest, so I greeted him warmly.

It was normal for the days to be a little warm, even in December, but this neighborhood was cold day and night. Seo-yeon didn't have a coat on and she seemed cold. We hurried inside.

"Honey, this house is so cozy!" Seo-yeon called to the husband.

Cozy? This barren house? Had they been living in a tent out in the wilderness? The husband showed Seo-yeon into the kitchen. She glanced around and placed her scarf on the couch. Then she took the picnic box that Kim was holding.

"Leave the kitchen to us," she said to me and Kim. "It's been a while for you two, why don't you catch up? Oh, and Inji, how do you feel about lamb? My husband likes it, so we decided on that."

"Yeah, lamb's good," I replied.

Seo-yeon rushed around as if she were the hostess and had arrived just after the guests. It felt like I had become the guest and had been told, *Feel free, make yourself at home*. I wasn't going to complain; I enjoyed having food cooked for me, but she was a bit of a peculiar guest. Seo-yeon and the husband went into the kitchen, and Kim and I sat down on the living room couch.

"I like the cherry blossom Christmas tree. Did you decorate it yourself?"

"I did it because I was bored, but I didn't have enough miniature bulbs."

"It's perfect as it is. I can sense the personal touch," he said with a chuckle.

As we chatted about the tree, my attention remained fixed on the kitchen. It looked like they were grilling meat in the oven. I could hear Seo-yeon talk, a bit of excitement evident in her voice, while the husband stayed silent, like he wasn't even there. I kept my gaze on the tree and inquired softly, "What's going on? If this continues, we might end up swapping spouses."

"That's something real couples do. If we do it, it's just group sex," Kim replied.

"What have I gotten myself into?"

"You still don't know? Those two used to be married. They lived together for three years, were married for three more, and now they're divorced," he added quietly, continuing to look at the tree. "How did you attach the miniature bulbs?"

"With cable ties. My husband did most of it."

The husband and Seo-yeon stood somewhere between friends and spouses. Apparently, Seo-yeon had joined NM first and later encouraged the husband to join too. You would think they were bound by fate or something. Maybe I was being a bit old-fashioned. If I were his real wife, I would have just given up and left them to be with each other with a *Goodbye and good luck*. I had no desire to stand on the sidelines and watch the stars align for them. Theirs wasn't the kind of relationship that was easy to resolve and be done with.

I didn't like how they seemed to have lingering ties to each other, which they refused to cut. It somehow bothered me more than an affair would have. I would have been annoyed even if they had met somewhere by sheer coincidence, but here they were intentionally organizing dinner parties together.

If I were his actual wife, I would have told them to have a nice dinner and left. Fortunately, Kim's presence made the situation somewhat better. It felt like some kind of sign that I had bumped into him the other day. It was my first time meeting him in several years, and now here he was in the house. It made me wonder what kind of connection we shared.

The husband called from the kitchen. Dinner was ready. *Yeah, all right,* I thought to myself, *if I weren't in NM, I would never have the opportunity to witness such a bizarre situation. Let's just enjoy this.*

Seo-yeon had brought a cake, some cookies, and four portions of lamb steak. It was all set together with the food the husband had prepared, so we had the appetizer, main, and dessert all laid out on the table. That way, we wouldn't have to go through the trouble of getting up to bring in each course. It was truly a party.

We clinked our wineglasses together and began to eat, helping ourselves to whatever we wanted. We had casual conversations about the neighborhood and collectively gushed about how striking the cherry blossom tree looked in the yard. As we started to feel the effects of the alcohol, our conversation moved to the subject of relationships, and then naturally landed on the subject of sex. When we had scraped the barrel of that conversation as well, it looked like we were going to just drink in silence. Only Seo-yeon, who was probably the most drunk out of the four of us, kept chattering away.

"Inji, this guy still has the habit of buying booze when he's drunk, right?"

"Yes."

"He told me that when he drinks, the bottles of alcohol start to look beautiful." She turned to the husband. "You just think all the bottles look so beautiful, don't you?"

The husband snickered. I had no idea that he bought alcohol because the bottles looked nice to him; the very idea was bizarre.

"We fought so much because of that," Seo-yeon continued. "Honey, has Inji ever gotten really mad and thrown a box of bottles away?"

"Not yet," replied the husband.

"You should fix that habit of yours before she starts to break and smash things, like I did."

The fact that she was casually calling the husband "honey" was getting on my nerves. It was clear that she still loved him. It was like Kim and I weren't even in the room or, even if we were, like we were just people there to work, no more and no less.

Seo-yeon kept glancing at the arm the husband had placed at the back of my chair. Maybe we should give her something to *really* look at. I leaned toward him and puckered my lips slightly. The husband met me in a light, easy kiss. I could feel Seo-yeon trying hard to pretend that she hadn't seen us.

"We fought so much when we were married. We probably didn't even fight that much when we first moved in together. Marriage just didn't suit us," Seo-yeon said coolly, as if she hadn't acted terribly in the past, and it was all long gone and forgotten. It was a tasteless gesture by someone who thought of herself as refined and elegant.

The husband didn't respond to each and every one of Seo-yeon's questions. However, he refilled her glass when it became empty, and handed her a napkin when she spilled a bit of food. He even briefly looked at her every time she called "honey," only to then turn away. Then Kim scolded Seo-yeon.

"Why do you keep calling him 'honey' when he's not your husband?"

"It's become a bad habit of mine. Sorry, Inji."

I had to laugh. *This is a bit of an awkward situation, isn't it, Seo-yeon?* I thought, *You've brought your own husband with you, but seeing your ex-husband's new wife for the first time isn't particularly pleasant, is it? You wanted to keep the monopoly on your husband forever, but that's not easily done. You're a guest, act like it. Don't pose like you own the place. That's how you win.*

"Wait, I haven't seen a single CD here! When I lived here, we were up to our elbows in CDs. Back then, I used to dream of living in a house where the walls had nothing on them. Honey, where are all the CDs?"

"In the studio on the second floor."

"I'll have to check it out later. Seems like I've got a love-hate relationship with CDs too."

I myself had never been upstairs to check out the recording studio. It wasn't that the husband had asked me not to; I'd just never thought to go up there. We didn't talk about work, so in my mind, that was his own, independent space.

"Now that I'm talking about it, I might as well go see it," announced Seo-yeon. "Inji and I are going to go check out the studio—can you please clean up here? That's okay, right, hon?"

I wondered which "hon" she was talking to. The husband, in order to get permission to enter his recording studio? Or Kim, who she was asking to clean up after her? Neither answered her. Seo-yeon stood, grabbing my arm.

"Let's go, they'll be fine."

The whole second floor was set up as a recording studio. The recording booth and control room were both elegantly decorated. The CD storage room was long and narrow, like a corridor, and looked like a small library. The racks were so fully packed that if I tried to take out one CD, a disk on either side would come out along with it. The indirect lighting above the racks gave the space a weird vibe. There were CDs of all kinds, ranging from music and movies to encyclopedias. The wall on the other side of the CD racks was filled with LPs. It was my first time seeing such a vast LP collection.

"Inji, your husband really likes Zalman King," said Seo-yeon.

"Is that the title of a movie?"

She laughed, explaining, "He's a pretty well-known director around these parts, if you know what I mean."

I had been thinking of *The Lion King* when I responded, but Seo-yeon was pointing to the area below her waist. She went straight into the little room next to the machine room. Inside, there was a Mac computer connected to two monitors and a keyboard. If there had been even scraps of a music score lying around, I might have been able to figure out what kind of music the husband made, but the place was spotless. Seo-yeon brought a CD in from the storeroom.

"Do you like Metallica? We're big fans—we used to listen to them constantly when we lived together. You should check out the original LP album later, it's a really good one. Let's go for 'Welcome Home' today—I haven't heard that one in quite some time."

Seo-yeon turned on the stereo in the corner of the room, inserting the CD. I hadn't even realized that it was a stereo; I thought it was just some kind of elongated audio device. The music boomed through the speakers. The volume must have been turned up quite high. When the song was at its climax, the shredding on the guitar was rapid, as though racing toward a finish line.

Ah, *Master of Puppets*. Metallica's third album. I could feel myself tearing up. I had first heard Metallica when I was in my final year of high school. I randomly came across the group late one night when I was listening to the radio, and then I later bought their CD. "Orion," that damn seventh track. I had never been interested in Western music and I didn't even know if Metallica was from the West, but the vaguely Western lyrical quality of their music brought my heart to a stop. To my ears, the guitar riff sounded like galloping horses. It was decisive, but passionate and mournful at the same time.

It was incredible how one song could be all of those things at once. I remembered showing Shi-jeong their music, excited at how amazing it was, only for her to ask me to turn the volume down. Metallica accompanied me through my final teenage years—just before my life turned into a wreck.

One of the men called from downstairs, "Come down when you're done listening. I'll bring out some beer."

"Sounds great, we'll be down in a second," I replied.

Downstairs, the kitchen was clean. Men seemed to be better at cleaning. They put in a good amount of effort and were quite thorough.

"Babe, you should go upstairs," I told the husband. "I think Seo-yeon is looking for an album."

"Which one?"

"A Metallica LP?"

"I'll head up. By the way, do you like Metallica?"

"I like Led Zeppelin."

The husband chuckled and headed upstairs. I sent the husband to be with Seo-yeon, to that empty spot beside her. I felt that it would fit him better than it did me. Having to listen to Seo-yeon rehash her old memories with my husband made me uncomfortable. She wasn't really likable, but I didn't necessarily hate her. Perhaps unsurprisingly, she was a bit catty, but to an understandable extent, and she seemed, in general, the type of woman to respect others. She must have really missed him.

Okay, Seo-yeon, you know what? That lamb steak was genuinely delicious, so I'll let you have this. I took a beer out of the fridge and handed it to Kim.

"Those two are probably going to be a while. We might as well start drinking."

Being together at the same place while each of us was on assignment felt a bit strange. Kim said that this was a first for him as well. While it was ridiculous that we had ended up meeting like this, it was even more ridiculous that the husband and Seo-yeon were able to get along on such friendly terms. What was this, some Hollywood flick? Sure, acting like good friends was better than behaving like enemies, but neither had the satisfaction that came with a clean break. Live-in partners for three years, then married for three, and then friends since. What a colorful life. It was like they decided, *Well, we tried doing the conventional thing for a while, now it's time for us to do what we want.* It wasn't a bad idea. A divorce wasn't really necessary when one person had been completely destroyed.

If things were bad enough that you had to hear people say things like, *You could get a divorce, it's justified at this point*, you were probably living in hell. Too many strangers became judges and jurors for other people's divorces, evaluating and assessing each aspect of their marriage. They kept score of everything, from infidelity and violence to household chores, parenting, income, denying sex, and so on. "Well, if things were that bad..." What an incredibly irresponsible and cruel thing to say. How bad was "that bad" exactly? Did having the same-sized plate mean you ate the same amount of food?

It wasn't the legal approval, but the approval of those around you that was more challenging to get. If you got sick of trying to live without people's acceptance and decided to just give up and tie a noose around your neck, judgment would arrive postmortem. Doing things like the husband and Seo-yeon wasn't bad, if the alternative was losing your life to the scrutiny of others.

Speaking of, those two were really taking their time

upstairs. What on earth were they doing up there? *They aren't re-creating a Zalman King movie in that soundproof booth, are they?* I thought. They were likely familiar with NM's matrimonial policy. They knew that infidelity led to a termination of contract. Were they looking to pay the equivalent of a whole new marriage in penalty charges? *What on earth is keeping them up there? Aren't they afraid of what I might make of it all?*

"What's Seo-yeon like?" I asked Kim.

"Just absolutely adorable," he replied. "What about your husband?"

"He's all right. Why are they still up there?"

As if summoned by my words, the two of them finally came down. I looked at their lips, wondering if they had kissed. When had Seo-yeon's cheeks turned that red? Where did she rub her cheeks? Those two, honestly…

"Dear, it's getting late. Let's go," Kim said to Seo-yeon.

"Sure. I feel so drunk, it's not even funny. Honey, call a taxi."

The husband searched for a taxi number on his cell phone. Seo-yeon kept making a fool out of me and Kim. *Whatever,* I thought, *do as you please. It must drive you crazy, right? But you're just friends now, what can you do? You can't have sex with him when you're just friends.*

Seo-yeon looked at me expectantly, but I made no move to ask her to stay, as was probably the polite thing to do. I just acknowledged her fatigue with a subtle smile. The husband received a call from the taxi driver, who said he was almost at the house, so we went outside. Having guests over was always so draining.

When I was a teenager, I used to dream about what my twenties would be like. Yet here I was, at the end of my twenties, and everything was such a mess. I could never have imagined that I would spend the last Christmas Eve of my twenties having sex with a man who invited his ex-wife over for dinner. The song "Orion" rang in my ears, even though it wasn't playing. I used to think that the song sounded vaguely like a man crying. Those were the days, days when I could become obsessed with some random song, and be content just listening to it all day.

"Are you okay?" the husband asked me. *It hurts*, I replied internally. It felt like I was hearing the faint sound of galloping hooves, fading away into the distance.

11

The husband made clear *kongnamul* soup for breakfast, to help with the hangover.

"You were really drinking wine like it was juice yesterday," he remarked.

"It was really good."

"Maybe I should change my habits to buying wine when I'm drunk."

"Sounds good. I'll do the dishes."

I cleared the table and washed the small number of dirty dishes.

You better not pout, I'm telling you why
Santa Claus is coming to town…

The husband brought a Bluetooth speaker from his studio and connected it to his iPad. He placed the small, round speaker right in the center of the table, as if it were a flower vase. The sound of a jazz musician singing a Christmas carol played through it. The song sounded light and cheery, but had a certain amount of gravitas to it. In my head, I pictured the singer to be a stately Black woman. It sounded like the voice of a Black person but with a Korean sentiment—as though a sadness permeated the seemingly cheery rhythm. I sang along, "'Santa Claus is coming to town.'" The husband walked around the yard, taking slow steps over the yellow grass, a cigarette in his hand. His fingers seemed so white. His slow movements were oddly well-timed, matching the rhythm of the carol.

A few days later, I met Kim at a café near the NM office. We usually tried to meet near the office when we were on assignments. That way, if someone from our married lives spotted us, we could use work as a reasonable explanation. Kim and I caught up with each other, though there wasn't any particular news either of us had to share. We spoke about some stuff that had happened at the office. It seemed like Kim had something to say to me, but he was having trouble bringing it up.

"Is there something you want to talk about?" I asked.

"I was just going to suggest that you take a bit of a breather. You looked tired that day."

His words served as a reminder of the nature of the profession we were in. We existed to serve our clients. We were meant to support them and prioritize their needs. We were essentially marriage professionals, tailor-made for our clients, and our labor was both physical and mental. However, I had apparently let things slip a bit and hadn't appeared very composed that day at the dinner party. Kim asked me if something was wrong, but I couldn't find the right words to explain.

"Inji, it's been about six years since you joined, right?"

"Yes."

"It's about time you get comfortable admitting that things are tough when they are. Terminating a contract feels hard the first time, but it becomes easier with each time you do it."

"Things are still fine with us."

"That's good. Nobody enjoys working, but you have to learn to make your work enjoyable."

Kim was very proactive. When he met a new spouse, he would quickly assesses them and form a plan for their marriage accordingly. He would laugh off minor conflicts, but if a partner was too uncooperative, he would terminate the marriage without hesitating. People didn't call him the Termination Expert FH for nothing. Kim was the type of person who really made his presence felt. For most other field employees, that was the opposite of what they wanted. They wanted to make their clients happy, but only to an extent. If the client didn't regret the marriage, that was good enough; any more would create too strong or lasting of an impact. Ideally, any lingering traces would be wiped away by the FW or FH that followed.

NM existed as a business to serve people who couldn't fit into the institution of marriage, those who wanted a marriage custom designed for them, and those for whom a conventional marriage wasn't possible. Most NM employees just passively accepted that the company's sole purpose was to improve these clients' quality of life with a more reasonable way of going about marriage, and fulfilled their roles as FW and FH accordingly. It felt a bit like being pulled out of a vending machine to quench a pressing thirst. The more fixed-term relationships you had, the emptier you felt.

Remarriage was extremely rare, since most clients didn't pass on the chance to be paired with a new spouse. Some would even start to develop a bit of an addiction. That was the inherent disadvantage of the contract marriage system. For the company, it was an unavoidable side effect, and it asked clients to be careful. However, it also served the company as an effective marketing tool. An increase in marriage contracts made it look like membership numbers were increasing too, which helped the company show that it could establish an even stronger presence in the market.

On a personal level, however, I was reaching my limit.

It felt like I was cutting bits of myself to sell. It was exhausting; I needed a sabbatical.

Kim and I continued to discuss the dinner party.

"My wife is a bit of a strange one," said Kim. "There's no denying it. Still, why were you acting so possessive?"

"Me?"

"You were acting jealous."

"When?"

Kim grinned as he sipped his coffee, while I bristled at his suggestion. What on earth would I be jealous of? I had just thought Seo-yeon was a bit obnoxious, that was all. Still, she was an NM client, so I kept my smile. Any kind of issue would only create problems for me, so I had nothing to gain by expressing my dislike for her.

However, according to Kim, that evening, the husband took up the role that had been my job to fulfill. He had been fairly accommodating of Seo-yeon's requests, but had also made it very clear that he was no longer her husband. Kim also mentioned having observed a similar interaction on a previous occasion, when the three of them had dinner together.

"I'd gone out that evening thinking we were going to meet a friend of hers, but turns out we were meeting her ex-husband," Kim recounted. "The two of them had decided to meet to discuss a store they co-owned. After the divorce, Seo-yeon left things up in the air, but your husband stepped in to clear it all up and gave her sole ownership. This apparently upset Seo-yeon, but your husband referred to it as a 'gift,' so she couldn't really say anything. When he was leaving, he said that he had plans with his wife."

"Wife? He meant me?" I replied.

"Yeah, I guess so. He said that he'd remarried, but I didn't know you were the wife. Anyway, after hearing that, Seo-yeon suddenly suggested throwing a party. She said she wanted to meet you, saying things like 'She must be really great, for you to have considered remarriage.' Honestly, I think she was a bit shocked. Seo-yeon had only suggested W&L to him as a joke, but it looked like he was actually enjoying it. I think that bothered her."

I found it ridiculous that she was acting so "shocked" when she was the one who had made the suggestion in the first place. It'd be nice if the husband could show me how much he was enjoying it too. When the woman you like was living on the first floor of the house, why would you leave her to go live on the second? I often went to bed alone, only to be startled in the middle of the night because the husband had decided to join me. It felt like he had only renewed his contract with me to get back at Seo-yeon. I was genuinely curious about why those two were the way they were, and Kim gave me a rundown on their situation.

The husband and Seo-yeon grew up in the same neighborhood. There, one kid was friends with another, who was friends with someone else, who was friends with the first, and so on. Usually, no one paid any attention to the friendships of little children, but in their neighborhood, complex social networks were put in place right from kindergarten. All the parents had their own connections with each other. If a relationship became strained, there was more to lose than gain. So, people were flexible—they were strict where need be, but they let sleeping dogs lie. They knew that any built-up animosity could burn a hole through important relationships, so they were careful.

"Gosh, that sounds exhausting," I said. "What's Seo-yeon like at home?"

"I've never met anyone with a personality like hers. She acts with such sincerity that it drives you insane."

"What does that mean?"

"Take the party that night as an example. She told me that she was going to go to your place and cook, to make things easier for you. How was I supposed to explain to her that not doing that would be the most helpful thing she could do, even if it meant you would starve of hunger? I honestly don't know if she's cunning or just naive. I thought I knew, but I'm not so sure," Kim explained. "You only ever have a vague sense of her intentions, so even though you get angry, you can't express that anger—since you can't point to a particular thing to get mad at. It's so frustrating."

"Exactly. So, are you going to end the contract this time as well, then?"

"The timing is tricky. Every time I feel like I'm going to end the marriage, things start to look okay, and I start to have doubts. I feel like your husband made the same mistake of hesitating too much, and then only narrowly escaped. In any case, I'm probably going to feel good for a bit, now that I've gotten all that off my chest," he said with a laugh.

We sat at the café, ordering one coffee refill after the other, as our conversation flowed on and on. We didn't need alcohol to have long chats that went on for hours. We were colleagues, but anyone who saw us would think we were dating, and you couldn't really blame them for it. We'd never held hands or been to each other's place, but we talked like we were lovers who couldn't get enough of each other. When company dinners would run late and we were both waiting for taxis to go home, he never chivalrously gave up the first taxi for me. If we were going in opposite directions, he'd just cross the street and catch a taxi without waiting to make sure I'd gotten one first. But it was completely appropriate for him to act this way. We had just the right balance of familiarity and distance, and I liked that. I think work would be quite painful for me if Kim wasn't around.

12

As soon the New Year's celebrations wrapped up, I switched my phone back on and turned on all its functions again. I called my mother and told her that I was going to meet up with the other colleagues who were in China. My mother disliked getting her news about me from other people. She was fine with knowing things that my brother or father hadn't been told yet, but she couldn't stand it when things were the other way around—in her world, she was supposed to be given priority, and only she could have access to confidential information. I went along with it, and gained my freedom by relieving her anxiety, a bit like wearing a revealing top, then putting a blazer over it.

"Don't just live on takeout, make sure to eat well," she told me.

It was a short phone call. Maybe I needed to just turn it off or take out its battery altogether. It made sense to just take the battery out, since I only used my work phone on assignments anyway. As soon as I had removed the back cover of my phone, it rang, startling me. It was Shi-jeong. Her timing was just impeccable.

"Check your emails! When did you start using your phone?"

"Just a second ago. Do you really have to start yelling the moment I pick up?"

I had only been checking my work email, and hadn't checked my personal inbox yet. My personal email was usually only for online shopping or website subscriptions, so it was always full of ads and I didn't see the point in checking it. Besides, it was too much work to log in, manually entering the username and password.

The longer I worked, the more my private life shrank. Sometimes, I wished that people would just forget about me altogether. *Are you married? What do you do for work?* I couldn't avoid their annoying questions. Even people in the family were the same. *You aren't married? I heard you work full-time.*

The only person who I kept beside me was Shi-jeong. She was the only reason that I sometimes missed my life outside of NM, and wanted to return to it. The outside world seemed like an illusion, but Shi-jeong's presence made it feel real again.

"I got a strange phone call from Tae-seong," said Shi-jeong.

"What?"

"It was like he didn't believe you were on a business trip. He was all intense and weird. I swear he wasn't that kind of person before. Everyone liked him because he was nice, like a friendly older brother or something. I guess you really have to wait and see with people, to know what they're really like. But anyway, nothing happened between you two, right?"

"Nothing."

"Are you coming home now?"

"I'm staying with some colleagues at the company resort."

"Keep in touch. We need to have dinner together to celebrate the New Year."

"Sure."

I hung up and turned off my phone. I wondered how Tae-seong was, if he was doing okay. Surely the company didn't still have him, right? It didn't seem like he knew anything about NM, and I was sure NM would be able to see that pretty clearly as well. I had reassured myself with that belief and then just moved on with my life, pretending like I had forgotten about him. It was the only way I could continue living my life as normal.

Tae-seong had made the mistake of going up to the NM house and pressing the doorbell. To the sensor, he was just a crazed, wild dog. Whether he was to be released, locked up, or euthanized was up to NM. I could just feel relieved knowing that he could no longer bother me, and then live the rest of my life in peace. Meeting him was never something I had agreed to in the first place; I had no interest in him, and I had never given him permission to be with me. I had made my feelings very clear to him, so this was all his own fault.

I brought out a bottle of beer from the fridge. It felt like I had sticky rice cake glued to the pit of my stomach. The husband came down from the second floor.

"You're having a beer at this hour?"

"I'm thirsty. Too much salt, I guess. Would you like one?"

"No, I'm good. You ski, right?"

"I snowboard. Why?"

"I'm working on this recording right now. It's fairly simple and should be done soon. Once I'm done, do you wanna go to a ski resort?"

"Sounds good. I'll go and get some snow gear while you're recording."

"You wanna go together?"

"Nah, I won't be able to focus if you're there."

I put the beer back in the fridge and went and grabbed my bag.

Shopping for clothes never took me too long. If I thought something looked good, I would just buy it. I had tried putting in a little more thought when I was picking things out, but I always just ended up with the same style anyway, so now I kept things simple. It was peak ski season, so the store was easy to spot. I walked straight in and immediately picked out a navy baseball-style jacket. I also bought underwear, ski goggles, a hat, and some gloves, all at the same store so I didn't have to go to any others.

My large shopping bag in hand, I walked to the first-floor coffee shop. It was dead quiet. But I decided to stay, and sat down at a corner table with a hot chocolate. Then, I called the director. As always, she inquired about my well-being in her typical cheerful tone.

"Inji, how are you? Is everything all right?"

"I'm well. I wanted to ask you about something."

"Shoot."

"It's about Om Tae-seong, the guy you took away last time. How is he? Is he doing okay?"

"Don't even go there," began the director. "I tried to send him away because he was freaking me out and couldn't get a grip on himself. That guy's a psycho. I don't know if it's because he's fearless or just plain stupid, but he's just so strange. I thought he might make a scene if we let him go, so I've put him in isolation."

"Where is he?"

I was shocked, and the director remained quiet for a while. It was a question that violated our company's security regulations.

"You know I can't talk about that. Why? What's going on?"

"He just suddenly came to mind, maybe because I just turned thirty. He really chased me around because he liked me so much."

"It's true, you do get all sentimental in your thirties. But it's just temporary. Try turning forty, then you'll miss your thirties. I'll handle everything, so don't worry, just relax."

"I'm going skiing with the husband tonight."

"Nice, worrying about stuff is inevitable, but you have to know how to enjoy yourself too. Have a great time."

Even my sweet hot chocolate left a bitter taste in my mouth. *Just what kind of a mess did you go and make there, Tae-seong?*

I rented a snowboard at the ski resort, and the husband came with his own skis. He had wanted me to buy my own snowboard as well, and suggested going to one of those fancy Gangnam department stores, but I didn't see the point when I was only going to throw it out after our marriage ended.

"Trends move so fast—even if I bought one, it would be out of style in no time."

"You could've at least bought some boots. Everyone else has boots—are you happy with what you have on?"

"It's not like I'm the only one wearing these shoes."

Back when I was a Japanese exchange student, Sapporo had the last natural ski resort. It was a place that retained as much of the natural terrain as possible. They did not smooth over the slopes, so I had a bit of a tough time navigating the hilly terrain. It was already several years ago now, but with that experience behind me, I was able to catch the lift up to the intermediate courses straight away. However, as soon as I ascended to the summit of the slope, my heart started to race. I was so nervous that I jumped off the lift extremely stiffly, as if I were a scarecrow with a frozen shoulder. It was a longer jump than I had expected. The slope looked like the snowy Alps, and I reasoned that, if things got too hard, I could always just sit on the board and slide down that way.

The husband started to prepare himself for the descent, warming up with small movements. I tried to ready myself as well, adjusting the bindings at my feet, but even when I had finished, I couldn't lift myself off the ground. My legs were trembling.

"Will you be okay?"

"I'll stumble around a bit, but then I'll be fine. You go ahead."

But he didn't; he waited for me. I was all the way up the slope, which meant that I had no choice but to go all the way down, even if I had to crawl my way there. I pushed myself off of the ground, stood up, leaned my hips outward, and went into a toe-side slide. In my nervousness, I was putting too much weight on my toes, which caused my calves to cramp up right from the get-go. I carefully moved to the side, muttering words of affirmation to myself: *Yes, that's right, you're doing great.*

If I could successfully make the heel-side sliding transition at the edge, I would complete the first S-turn. But I was too slow, and my snowboard flew through the snow as if it were a pile of autumn leaves. I skidded down quite rapidly, which was something most proper skiers would hate to see. When a snowboard skidded through the snow on a slope, it created an icy surface, making it very slippery and dangerous for any skiers that followed. I really needed to pick up more speed, so I leaned forward to draw myself ahead.

But suddenly, the edge of the slope was right in front of me, and I didn't have to time to calculate my next

move. A skier was quickly approaching me, going reck-
lessly fast, and I rushed to avoid them. *Fuck.* I muttered
several expletives as I focused on turning away. I had to
use my ankles to change the angle of my feet so I could
turn, but my knees were too stiff, and I tumbled over. It
was a miracle that I had stayed up for so long in the first
place. The husband put his hand under my arm, helping
me up. I stood up like a scarecrow, with both feet still
attached to the board.

"Do you want me to go with you and hold you from
behind?"

"I think I'll be fine now, after that run."

"If you have trouble, just let me know and I'll help
you out."

I jumped in place to shake off the snow piled on my
board, preparing to have another go. When else would
I get a chance to play around in the snow like this? This
intermediate-level course was a bit too long though.
Not too far ahead, I fell again, this time so hard that the
husband shuddered. He didn't ask if I was okay because
he knew I probably wasn't. He continued to silently follow me from behind, like some sort of collision preven-
tion officer.

Still, having fallen a few times seemed to have paid off.
My senses began to come alive. I descended smoothly, even

swaying back and forth a little, enjoying myself. *That's more like it*. My knees and waist started to fall in sync.

The husband skied down with me, without using his poles this time. Show-off, was he an instructor or something? I went a bit faster as I approached the center, which just happened to lead to a sudden slalom. I almost ran into some poor skier, who yelled out expletives and veered off the path. The husband, this time using poles, followed suit. His posture was that of a perfect skier. It was as if the skis were an extension of his body. It was the sexiest I'd seen him since we met. Anyway, I soon had to tell him to get out of my way, because I had almost run into him more than once.

"You're quite good," he praised me, smiling. Now that I was in the flow of it, I took two more turns on the intermediate course. Then, for the husband's sake, we went on the advanced course and I barely made it down, heart in throat. Understandably, the advanced course was not easy to conquer.

I ate some fish cakes at the snack bar before leisurely completing a final descent on the intermediate course. Having fun in the snow had made my chest feel less stuffy. I had a constantly runny nose, which was a bit of an embarrassment, especially in front of the husband, but it was all worth it. I was glad we'd made the trip.

13

I always enjoyed eating some pork belly after a ski trip, so we went to a restaurant near our place that specialized in it. Eating pork belly and soju after a few days of skiing was the best. My entire body ached like someone had beaten it to a pulp. So I had made up my mind to eat to my heart's content, as a reward. I took a shot of soju, and it burned my throat.

"When did you start skiing? It's honestly the sexiest thing I've ever seen you do," I said to the husband.

"Since I was pretty young. Who have you been snowboarding with this whole time?"

"I've had a snowboarding partner since high school."

"You went to an all-girls high school, right?"

"Why, are you worried that if it was co-ed, I would

have been snowboarding with a guy? Would that be so wrong?"

"No, it's not that. It's just that you don't talk much about your friends."

Really? I thought, *The only person you've ever introduced me to is your ex-wife. We've never spoken to each other about the people in our life—there's no need to start now. You have this friend, and that friend, and that other friend from that place, right? Well, so do I. We are each entangled in webs of social relations—can't we just stick to our own?*

When it came to the husband and me, I wanted us to be two people who had met by chance on a cold day, and simply shared the heat of our bodies for a moment. When our marriage contract expired, we would need to meet other people. If there was too much heat now, in this moment, those that were yet to come would feel too cold. I quickly changed the subject.

"I heard you like Metallica?" I asked the husband.

"Who, me?"

"Oh, you don't?"

"It's Seo-yeon who likes Metallica. I'm more into Led Zeppelin, like you."

I see, so that's how it is. Seo-yeon, that little— It looked like Seo-yeon had been trying to use me to get the husband thinking about her. If she liked him that much, why even agree to a divorce? That hurt. I should have just continued to think of Metallica as the husband's favorite band and played their music loudly from the speakers. That's what she wanted, didn't she? Then the husband would probably think of her.

But would the memories he thought of be good ones? What if the husband was trying really hard to forget Seo-yeon but I kept reminding him of her through the music and driving him insane? I could imagine him finally stumbling upon an oasis after wandering through the desert, only to see Seo-yeon shimmering in the haze of heat. *Shit, this oasis is just a mirage*, he would lament. It was like he was caught between a rock and a hard place. The two of them were really…something.

Also, what was up with that whole Zalman King thing? Was it like a tip for my sex life with the husband, a reward for playing Metallica for her? Whatever it was, it was a bit insulting. Why was she putting herself into the bedroom affairs of someone else's marriage? I guess it was her way of saying that this wasn't "someone else's" marriage. I was having sex with the husband because I had been granted permission by his ex-wife. The thought drove me crazy, but I couldn't even say anything to her because she was a client.

No matter how angry I got, I had no choice but to just hold it in. Seo-yeon and I stood in completely different positions in this situation, so it was inevitable that one of us was going to be miserable. I understood why people tried desperately to make sure they were the ones with good standing, with all the advantages.

I was really curious about what the husband and Seo-yeon's marriage had been like. Looking at the husband's skills in the bedroom, he was definitely no Zalman King. I wanted to try and get a sense of things.

"Do you like Zalman King?" I asked. "I think he's pretty good, so I've seen a bit of his work in the past."

"Oh yeah? I like him too. Did you watch his final film?"

"No, I still haven't watched it."

I've barely known him a few days and now you're telling me he's already retired? I suddenly found myself with a new fondness for this spirited, eccentric virtuoso. The husband watched me intently. It looked like he was waiting for me to speak, but I had nothing to say. It would be weird if I just kept saying that I liked Zalman King, and then ended the conversation there. I would have discussed King's movies with him if I had seen any of them, but I hadn't.

My husband was indecisive and didn't stay at anything long enough for it to be satisfying. He was always caught between doing it and not doing it, jumping and not jumping, doing one thing or doing another. *Is that what King's movies are like?* I wondered.

The husband savored a shot of soju. He chuckled slightly and remarked that our tastes were quite similar, even though I actually like Metallica more than Led Zeppelin, and melodramas more than porn. While other films were made to portray the spectrum of human emotion, the main goal of porn was just sex. That clear-cut simplicity of it was nice, but it just wasn't my cup of tea. It seemed like the husband and I were similar but, at the same time, very different.

"Do you wanna watch it later?" my husband asked.

"Watch what?"

"King's final work."

I was taken aback. I could barely remember the last time I had even watched porn. Back in our university days, Shi-jeong had brought a Japanese movie that had won a bunch of awards at an international film festival. It was a movie about a woman who was so obsessed with sex, it was all she thought about, day and night, no matter where she was. In the latter half of the movie, she cut a man's genitals off and kept them, as she had not come across any genitals that suited her sexual preferences for quite a while. No matter how you looked at it, it was porn, but Shi-jeong was adamant that it was based on a true story.

"So, it's real-life porn then," I said.

"Just look at how well-made it is!" she insisted.

"So, it's really well-made porn."

"Don't just look at the genitals, look at the film as a whole."

"The whole thing is just that crazy bitch playing with the genitals!"

After we had exchanged of our views on the movie, we stopped watching it. At the time, I had been in a passionate romance with a senior who worked with me for the school paper, and I think Shi-jeong had been feeling a bit neglected, which was why she brought over the movie. Maybe she was trying to tell me to cut the balls off my man. He and I got caught doing the deed just once at the school newspaper office, and from that point on, Shi-jeong suspected that we were always up to the same thing every time we would disappear. Even when I denied it, Shi-jeong did not believe me.

Okay then, I thought, *let me really play the part*. I pulled together my entire sex-related vocabulary to ostentatiously elaborate on the gravity-defying extreme pleasure we were engaged in. I was so clearly lying, but Shi-jeong bought it all. At that time, I received as much criticism as I did love from the newspaper boyfriend. From the way I treated my sources to my use of punctuation, he said that my journalism skills had a long way to go.

Contrary to what Shi-jeong may have believed, our relationship didn't just consist of passionate romance.

We had sex, but we were both young and awkward and weren't always sure whether we were doing it right. We didn't even know what "extreme pleasure" was supposed to feel like. We just liked being together. Now, instead of a school newspaper boy, the man I was with was a virtuoso. Why did I keep finding myself in unfamiliar situations where I ended up being the seasoned, experienced expert? The alcohol was starting to hit me.

"Today was kinda tiring. Let's watch it another day."

My husband topped up my empty glass. It looked like he was in a good mood.

"In your profile, you said that your hobby was making homemade albums. I haven't seen you make them."

"You said that you're a composer, but I haven't seen you write a single song."

"Touché."

My father worked at a manufacturing company for office equipment. Since he worked there, there was always equipment like binders, laminators, and cutters at home. I would get cards or fallen leaves for fun and coat them several times over, then bind them together. After being bound, they look like regular notepads. I made little gifts by printing out friends' photos, laminating and binding them. It was obviously not something that was really expensive or took an incredible amount of skill, so it was a gift that was easily given and easily received. The equipment didn't take up much space, so it was easy to store.

I also liked the analog nature of laminating each piece by hand at the stationery store. Now, people could just scroll and look at photos on a screen, but it just wasn't the same as doing something by hand. The larger the memory storage, the more photos a person would take. But both the person taking picture and the people in the picture were indifferent to the process. They didn't feel like memories being made; they felt more like pieces in a large collection of data. I had made more than twenty copies of my father's mountain-climbing club album. The members of the club loved it so much that they even gave me some money to thank me.

The alcohol seemed to have boosted the husband's mood.

"Why don't we make an album?" he asked.

"But then it'll all just become a memory," I replied.

My husband nodded his head placidly.

"There's nothing quite like a bottle of soju for when you need to open up," he remarked, "I wonder why that is?"

"Soju is easy," I explained. "It's not like wine, where even the glass has to be fancy. You have to know where it was made, the year, the grade and batch of grapes used, and only then can you look like you know your shit. When you're being so formal about everything, it's hard to talk about what's on your mind. I saw this French movie once where the main character bought wine from a supermarket and drank it straight out of the bottle. The way they drank it, it looked so satisfying. They just popped it open and gulped it down. I think people in Korea make such a fuss about drinking wine. Everyone's a fucking connoisseur."

"Did you just say 'fuck'?" asked the husband.

Oops… Looked like I was so drunk that my habits from the outside world were slipping in. I never had something like this happen before, even when I had chugged wine like it was juice.

"Really human of you to say something like that," the husband said, laughing.

"Yeah, I'm like that. Waiter," I called, "another bottle of soju please!"

"On another note," said the husband, "you don't have anything to say about Seo-yeon?"

"Yeah, nothing about her really stood out to me. I thought she was all right. What was it about her that put you off?"

"Just trivial things. For example, when she speaks, her tongue doesn't hit the roof of her mouth."

"What?"

"I've heard that for most people, you can't talk without

hitting the roof of your mouth or touching your upper teeth. Seo-yeon talks as though her tongue is glued to her bottom teeth. She speaks like she's holding a ball of air in her mouth."

I could barely hold back my laughter. How could *that* be something to get pissed off about? I had assumed that was just how she talked, and didn't think twice about it. But once that man latched on to something, it really became an obsession. Despite this, Seo-yeon still loved him and wanted to feel butterflies when she was with him.

And so, she made the mistake of introducing the husband to NM, assuming that being in contract marriages would leave him no time to find a woman to actually fall in love with. But love does not need a long time to occur. It can happen in an instant, and it is powerful. You can resist it for a long, long time, but it has the force to break you in a single second.

Of course, the husband wasn't going to get that kind of force from me. There was only the slightest possibility. And yet, Seo-yeon felt threatened by even that slim potential. It made my head hurt. If the husband disliked women who spoke with their tongue stuck to their bottom teeth, maybe he should just go out with women who could contort their tongue into only touching their upper teeth.

"Let's get going," I said.

★ ★ ★

I got up from my seat. My body was already in pain; it had been too long since I had been skiing. I had discovered a lot of new things about the husband today. He had an unexpectedly innocent side to him. I really wanted to leave, but the husband was still in the restaurant. Maybe he had gone to the toilet. I took a peek inside. *Oh gosh, why is he like that?* was my reaction when I spotted him.

The husband was standing in front of the beverage fridge and was stuffing a black plastic bag with bottles of alcohol. His drinking habit had kicked in. Actually seeing it in action, I was left kind of speechless. He was more clearheaded than I was, and he looked completely sober.

I went back into the restaurant. The husband placed the plastic bag on the counter. It felt so stupid to me; buying alcohol here was so much more expensive than buying it at a store. I counted the bottles and there were twelve of them altogether. The restaurant owner tallied the bill on the calculator. I looked at the husband and remarked, "They have soju here that's from South Jeolla."

The owner handed over the card and the receipt and replied, "My hometown is in that region so I keep them in stock."

His hometown wasn't too far from where my parents

and brother lived. The husband nodded in response, and we left the restaurant. If he had bought twelve bottles of just the South Jeolla soju, that might have made sense to me. That could be explained as an impulse buy, because the bottles just happened to catch his eye. But the twelve bottles he had bought included some of the regular soju we had been drinking with dinner. I couldn't say anything to him then—you could only talk to someone about fixing their drinking habits when they were sober.

The husband carried the twelve bottles of alcohol and walked alongside where the spring onion patches would be, had the ground not been left barren by the winter cold. I walked slowly and steadily beside him. I wondered what the criteria were for deciding if someone was drunk. The thin, slanted moon up ahead looked more drunk than the husband beside me.

Or maybe he just seemed sober to me because I was drunk. I had never seen anyone look the way he did when drunk.

"Need any help with the bags?" I asked.

"It's all right."

"Were the bottles really that pretty?"

"You're the one that's pretty."

He really was drunk.

14

The husband and I seemed to have become closer since our ski trip. I certainly felt more comfortable around him. Our life looked like a single basket shared by chicken eggs and duck eggs—similar yet different. However, I did not want to close the gaps between us by force. If you get too emotionally attached to an impossible task, all you are left with is resentment. Trying to force things can also lead to arguments and, in the end, hurt.

The husband seemed to be on the same page, as he didn't force me to be like him. He acted like an ocean wave, drawing close and then receding, with a consistent rhythm. And yet, the one thing he adamantly refused to let go of was his demand for a handmade photo album. I couldn't understand why he was making such a fuss over a silly little photo album, but in the end, I threw in the towel. He just had to have it.

The husband brought out a camera. Sure, we could take pictures now, but they would stay with us even after the contract ended—had he thought about how awkward it would feel then? You couldn't fully get rid of pictures, even if you tried to shred or burn them. Photos stay, carved in your mind, like etchings on stone.

The husband showed me his antique-looking Olympus Pen EE-3, a childhood gift from his father. I assumed he was attached to it because it was his first camera. The Pen EE-3 was a small but efficient camera that took seventy-two photos with a thirty-six-exposure film. The photos were slightly low in resolution, but the imperfection gave them a unique, vintage charm. The camera was old, but obviously well looked after.

"Mr. Camera never gets sick. He's healthy as a horse," the husband said.

"He's cute, like a little toy. Let me take some photos of you."

"Let's take some together."

"I don't like being photographed."

I asked the husband to hand me the camera. It was difficult to figure out how to take a picture with its narrow viewfinder. I framed the husband roughly in what seemed to be the center of the shot and pressed down on the shutter button. The shutter made a rather disappointingly soft clicking sound. The husband and I moved around the house as I took photos of him, but then a red indicator light came on. I asked the husband why, and he affectionately responded that Mr. Camera was sticking out his tongue in displeasure because the room was too dark. He then got up to pull the blinds all the way up, letting in warm sunlight to fill the space. And indeed, Mr. Camera took his tongue back in.

I started taking photos of the husband again. He posed, smiling gently, then frowning slightly, and looked good doing both. He turned toward the camera, looking straight at it, but even then looked natural, and laid-back.

As I kept taking photos, I was reminded that I had hardly been photographed since Coming of Age Day, back when I had just turned nineteen. I struggled with having my picture taken, even if it was just for an ID card. It was because I hadn't been able to move on from Hye-yeong's passing. Shi-jeong and I had deliberately repressed her memory, and bringing it to the surface now was too painful.

"Would you turn around slightly?" I asked the husband, so I could take some pictures from a different angle. *Click, click, click…* I snapped away, taking picture after picture of the husband.

★ ★ ★

Shi-jeong, Hye-yeong, and I were like the Three Musketeers throughout high school. Then, one day, the morning after we had just celebrated Coming of Age Day, Hye-yeong died. Her death was completely un-expected, and she was the one who had organized the party in the first place. When Shi-jeong and I had arrived at the motel for the party, everything had already been prepared. Hye-yeong had come earlier to put out food, including a cake. The room was decorated with red rib-bons and balloons hanging from the ceiling. There were party hats, and even a karaoke machine. To us, motels were like a secret hiding place, where we were free to do whatever we wanted in complete privacy. So, we shaped our hair with whipped cream and dressed up in white slips to play at Marilyn Monroe, we ran around throw-ing tissue paper in the air, and we even sang Christmas carols together. By the end, with tissue paper and fruits and all kinds of food strewed across the floor, the room was in such a state that anyone who saw it would assume we had been high on something all night.

Shi-jeong was asleep next to me, but Hye-yeong was nowhere to been seen, although her bag and phone were still in the room.

Assuming that Hye-yeong had just gone out to get some fresh air, I woke Shi-jeong up and started cleaning the room. However, Hye-yeong didn't show up, not even when we were supposed to check out of the motel. She was usually a good kid but, for some reason, she would always end up doing something weird on big, special occasions. Shi-jeong and I packed up and waited for Hye-yeong in front of the motel. I think we waited for about an hour, after which we started calling people, and eventually decided to call her mother as well.

"Did anything happen last night?" I remember her mother asking.

"We were just having fun, but we might have gone a little overboard," I responded.

"There was an accident this morning."

Hye-yeong, who we had spent so much time waiting for, was waiting for us as a photograph at the funeral home.

It was a quiet funeral; there was no wailing or crying. Hye-yeong's mother sat still as a gravestone, holding on tightly to a handkerchief in her hand. A long time ago, my mother had told me that a mother had to choose when to be ill, so that it suited her child's plans. She told me that there had been times when she was sick, but pretended not to be, because it was a busy time for me or my brother. It wasn't like anyone would judge her for falling ill, but it was a mother's nature to endure her sickness so as not to disturb her child.

That day at the funeral, Hye-yeong's mother looked extremely ill. It felt like she was now letting herself be properly ill, since her daughter no longer had any plans that could be disturbed. When she looked at Shi-jeong and I, her eyes seemed to be asking, *What happened?* We probably looked clueless in response. But, since we were guilty of negligence, of being fast asleep in bed while our friend went out all alone early in the morning, we apologized, over and over again.

The tears came flowing when Hye-yeong's father invited us to the dining part of the funeral hall to eat before we left. I had so many questions. What time did Hye-yeong leave the motel? Why did the accident happen in front of her home instead of the motel? What kind of accident made for a funeral so deserted and lonely?

The tears Shi-jeong and I shed were all the tears shed that day. That was how sad and dry the funeral was. As Hye-yeong's father showed us to our seats, we ate with our backs against two ladies. There were so few people that the staff there had nothing to do, no one to serve, and so they just sat on their chairs, staring blankly into the distance.

"How did it happen?" one of the ladies asked the other.

"You heard her. Her airway got blocked because she was vomiting during her sleep. That's what we've been told, so that's what happened—there's no need to ask any more questions."

"It's like if a baby died as it was asleep on its stomach. I just don't know what to say."

So, Shi-jeong and I essentially found out how Hye-yeong died by overhearing a conversation between two ladies. Since that was all the information we heard, we had no choice but to accept it. Hye-yeong died because her airway got blocked.

People could die that way, but I was not convinced that a blocked airway had caused my friend's death. Shi-jeong also looked like she had her doubts. We didn't have any definitive proof, but we were probably thinking the same thing. It was a suicide. That was the idea on our minds, making us unable to speak. The night of our frenzied party was the eve of Hye-yeong's death.

It made no sense. But that's what had been said, so that's what we had to accept.

A few days after the funeral, Hye-yeong's mother invited us home. I thought that she may have decided to reveal the truth just to us or, alternatively, she wanted to hear the truth from us. However, her mother mentioned nothing about the cause of death. She brought us to Hye-yeong's room, telling us to grab something to remember her by.

In all honesty, I had already drifted apart from Hye-yeong, even before that fateful night. Also, my room was already filled with things to remember her by. But I couldn't not take anything, not when Hye-yeong's mother was tailing us with her eyes. She would lock her eyes on everything I touched. It was a lot of pressure; I felt like I was being asked to give my condolences even to the objects in Hye-yeong's room.

At that moment, I saw Hye-yeong's album. I flipped through the photos taken in high school one by one and realized that she didn't have any photos of me. It was like she had removed not just pictures of me, but any pictures that I might have appeared in, including pictures with her, and even group pictures of our entire class. I also couldn't see the handcrafted album I had made her back when we were still good friends.

I wondered why, but I could not ask, because Hye-yeong was dead. I felt like I had been murdered by being eliminated from her photo album. I wanted to get out of the room. I randomly took out a golden button from the jewelry box on the dresser. I had no idea why Hye-yeong had kept such a useless button in her jewelry box, and I didn't particularly want to know. I just wanted to get the hell out of there. I remembered that Shi-jeong took fluffy gloves.

As I exited the room, Hye-yeong's mother looked at my hand.

"Is that all?"

"I'm going to use it as a pendant."

Hye-yeong's mother regarded me coolly, as if I hadn't met her expectations. Her eyes seemed to be saying, *You both should be a lot sadder, don't you think?* I hated it.

I heard the chime bell on the laundry machine ring. The washing was done.

"Saved by the laundry machine! You just kept going and going—what do you need so many pictures for?" the husband said.

"Not all of them will be good, you know."

I returned the camera to the husband and went to the laundry machine, pulling out the washed laundry and putting it into a basket. The best thing about this house was being able to hang laundry in the front yard. The clothes would sometimes freeze if it got too cold, but they usually dried well under the winter sun. They would smell different if I hung them to dry in the balcony instead, even if I used the same detergent.

I saw the husband standing in front of the living room window, holding the camera, but I pretended not to see him and starting hanging the laundry. I wasn't too bothered by him; I would only be a part of the larger scenery after all. But I still turned around, so that my face wouldn't be in the photo. I flapped the clothes so vigorously that my whole body shook, and looked at the front gate. I felt like someone was standing behind it. I had been feeling that way often lately. So, I decided that today was going to be the day. I left the empty basket next to the laundry machine and took a deep breath. I was going to do it; I was finally going to talk to the husband about it.

"Hey, honey, wanna have a beer?"

"Sounds good."

I brought in the beer, along with some light snacks. I wasn't sure how to begin. The more experienced I got, the harder it became to trust clients. Clients worked very closely with the company. They could get a FW or FH replaced at the snap of a finger. If anything went wrong, I would have to pay for the breach of contract and leave the company.

Still, this had to be done. I couldn't keep letting the pressure on my chest suffocate me any longer. I was already suffocating because of Hye-yeong. *Talk first, think about the consequences later*, I told myself. I took a sip of beer to help with the dryness in my throat. Then, I asked, "Have you heard anything about Tae-seong, by any chance?"

"Very briefly. The company seems to have isolated him. Why?"

"I'm just asking. That's harsh, though."

"If a dog bites a person, you have to kill it."

"I hope you're joking. It's just a poor little dog."

"Is it okay for 'just a poor little dog' to bite a person?"

The husband didn't care what kind of a relationship Tae-seong and I had. To him, Tae-seong was just a wild dog who had barged into his home, so he was okay with Tae-seong being violently captured. I wished I could also be that indifferent.

I found it hard to figure out the husband. There was such a huge difference in how he treated some people versus others. He was kind to his select few, and that kindness had clear, firm boundaries. He never got too worked up about anything. Even to me, he would sometimes say the coldest things calmly, and with a smile. The husband was like a tourist in a safari, chancing upon humans in the wild every now and again, and observing them from a distance, fascinated. Still, surely reckless killing was unacceptable to him.

"Should we visit him?" I asked.

"Why?"

"I'm connected to the whole thing. It just leaves a bad taste in my mouth. The problem is that you can only make those kinds of visits if you're a manager or higher."

"Promotions are given for a reason. The higher you go, the quieter you have to be. You don't need that kind of headache without the promotion."

"I don't see myself being promoted to the director level, so why not get a taste of it? But I don't know if I could do that without going through the company."

"I'm sure it's not impossible. Do you want to see him?"

"As long as you're okay with it."

"How much do you trust me?"

"About as much as I can, as your wife."

"Okay then, let's take a short trip."

The husband held up his beer, and I held up mine to his. We clinked our glasses together. I had never liked Tae-seong. I had rejected him, again and again, and when I realized that he just wasn't going to accept my refusal, I reached out to NM for help. But before he started showing up at NM to see me, I had interpreted his gestures as well intended.

I thought Tae-seong was trying to be kind to lonely little me, that he was the kind of person who was stubborn, and hell-bent on doing what he wanted, but out of kindness. But I hated that. I had never liked people who used their kindness to do whatever they wanted, knowing that you wouldn't be able to refuse. These people would corner you with kindness and leave you no room to breathe. They also thought their idea of kindness was everyone else's idea of kindness. I just didn't like them.

Sure, I had maybe been especially aggravated by Tae-seong because of the life I lived and how important privacy was to my job. But now, I fully understood that Tae-seong had not been acting out of kindness. Since I knew that, I should have been relieved that he was gone, but I couldn't help the weird, heavy feeling in my heart. Tae-seong's voice asking, *Why do you hate me?* still rang in my ears. His theatrical bubbliness also stuck with me. Tae-seong looked like a child who forced himself to smile while getting beaten up. I wondered what had made him that way. Tae-seong had told me that he had a younger sister. She was probably waiting for him to come home.

Despite my hatred of him, I would honestly have preferred it if he was just out there, living his life well. Whether I liked it or not, I was a part of this. I wished I could run away and escape the confusing guilt that had stuck itself to me.

15

The husband found Om Tae-seong in a prayerhouse in a small city outside of Seoul. He had not found this place through the company, and I was surprised by his ability to dig out information. I wondered how he had found the place, when it operated in complete secrecy. It had been so easy for him that it made me wonder whether I had dug my own grave.

Not that I had especially trusted the husband. Had there ever even been a time where my trust hadn't been broken before the end of a relationship? It hurt less when you started off without trusting the other person. If my grave had been decided already, I was going to be found out even if I tried to hide.

The flight from Gimpo Airport took about an hour. Our taxi drove through the airport exit, entered the city, and, after passing through several neighborhoods, began to follow a winding mountainous road. The remote ranges weren't particularly high, but they were dense and lush. The taxi driver stopped the car where the husband asked him to. We were surrounded by motels. It was a pretty good location for a motel, deep in the ranges where the view was nicest.

We went into one of the more isolated motels. There was a lobby with coffee and snacks but no front desk in sight. There had been three entrances that looked similar, so we were confused as to which the main entrance was. Just when I was starting to think it might be a self-check-in motel, I heard someone call us. An attendant was sitting behind a small window that looked like an old theater box office. The husband went up to her.

"Check-in is at 7:00 p.m., checkout is at 12:00 noon tomorrow," the attendant said.

"Is it possible to check in now?"

"Yes, at an extra ten thousand won per hour."

"That's fine, we'll go with that."

The room we were using was on the fifth level. There was a Jacuzzi right next to the bed, even though the room had a separate bathroom. The room also had a state-of-the-art sound bar below a wall-mounted TV, and two desktop PCs sitting side by side. The combination of the crimson wallpaper, dim lighting, and the technology created a bizarre atmosphere. It was this weird hybrid of a steamy love motel and business hotel. It looked like it would be suitable for a couple in neatly pressed uniforms to come in and have sex. However, the bed was a problem. There was a hard plastic layer under the white cotton bedspread. The structure had no warmth to it, making it feel like lying on the bare floor. It was going to be difficult to get a good night's sleep. The husband smirked.

"I bet there aren't many people coming here just for some decent shut-eye."

"I get doing what you came here to do, but you still need a good night's sleep."

"Well, if you do it right, you're definitely going to sleep well."

It was like the husband was incapable of getting nervous. He was acting like we'd just come here on a short holiday to get some fresh air. The husband seemed very relaxed, so I guessed that Om Tae-seong was doing better than I thought. I felt slightly relieved. There was nothing much to do, so I looked around the room and opened a paper bag that was placed next to some towels. It contained disposable toiletries, a toothbrush and toothpaste, and two condoms. The atmosphere of the room was so inescapably charged that if you really got into it with enough gusto, just two condoms might not be enough.

I put down the paper bag and opened the window. I thought I would be able to see the prayerhouse because we were higher up, but instead I was met with the sight of another motel. Not a single room had its windows open. I decided that it must be because of the cold weather and dismissed any other, dirtier thoughts.

"Honey, is that place far from here?"

"No, it's down the road where we got off the taxi earlier."

The place was located behind the motel. The sign on the outside read Sodam Farm, but there was apparently both a farm and a prayer center inside. The husband and I rested for a while before leaving our motel room. We passed by a youthful couple in the hallway. Either they were teenagers posing as twentysomethings, or twentysomethings acting like teenagers. I hoped they made sure to use the condoms provided in their room.

We arrived where the taxi had stopped earlier. Sodam Farm was just inside a narrow road to the right. The arched iron gate complemented the surrounding scenery. The gate's bars were widely spaced, and its arches were gentle and elegant. The small handwritten wooden sign looked nice too.

Two young women came up to the gate and posed in front of it, using a selfie stick to take a bunch of pictures from different angles. We were only able to go inside the farm once the two women went up the path. Through the window outside, I saw an interior decorated with various bonsai trees, a leather sofa, and a metal desk—the kind of furniture commonly used in offices. A yellow kettle sat on a stovetop. Just looking in made me feel warm and cozy. But there were no people in sight.

The husband rang the bell on the grille under the sign. When he rang the bell a second time, I saw a man come in through the back door of the office. He looked at us through the window. The husband pressed the bell one more time, and the man finally came out of the office through the front door. He looked to be in his early forties and was wearing a worn green parka with dirty sleeves. The husband immediately asked for the custodian, without even introducing himself.

"What brings you here?"

"Let them know that Elder Choi sent me."

The man led us into the office and left through the back door. The earthy scent of Solomon's seal tea wafted from the kettle above the stove. Korean teas like cassia seed, corn, Solomon's seal, and brown rice tea were on display inside a glass cabinet. A few moments later a meek man in his midsixties came in through the back door.

He was the custodian, and he wore the same parka as the man who had welcomed us. He looked unimposing, like a kind old man, maybe because of his outfit and the fanny pack he wore around his waist. He poured some tea from the kettle as soon as he came in.

"Please, have a drink, it's cold out there today."

The custodian placed the teacup on the table. It was a sturdy earthenware cup that paired well with the tea and seemed like it had also been made on the farm.

"How's the tea?" the custodian asked.

"Delicious," the husband responded.

"That's what everyone says about our tea. By the way, how is Elder Choi?"

"I've heard he's staying healthy. Although I haven't been able to see for myself," the husband answered.

"Yes, he's a tough one. Even at his age, he still manages to chew the cartilage in his food. So, what can I do for you?"

"We need someone."

"For what purpose?"

"Right now, we need someone to guard the mountain cabin. A mild-mannered male in his early thirties. Is that possible?"

"Seems like the age is important?"

"Such are the circumstances."

The custodian nodded. I held the teacup but I couldn't

bring myself to drink. Human trafficking. These people were having a conversation without batting an eye, as if they weren't talking about people. They might as well have been saying, *"I need a dog." "Oh, for what purpose?"*

"We do have someone, but well, I think you should see him for yourself."

"Can we see him right now?"

"Yes, I'll show you the way."

We followed the custodian out the back door. The area behind the compound was beautiful, and the surrounding trees and vegetation had all been preserved. To the right, there was a small brook that had dried up, but looked like it would be a great spot for picnics in the summer. The prayerhouse was some way farther down, where they had built stairs by driving wooden logs into the ground.

The custodian cautioned me to be careful as I descended in my heels. I watched as he opened a heavy iron door, its thick metal blocking the way forward. It was immense, and anyone would strain under its weight to push it open. We followed the custodian inside. The metal made no grating sound, but the thud of the door closing was echoed by the thud of my heart dropping. Had I just entered my final resting place?

Outside of NM, Om Tae-seong's existence wasn't particularly noteworthy. If you are told not to do something, you should not do it, and if you're told that's how it is then you should just accept that. You should not resist or make a fuss. And yet, here I was. *Damn it.* I found myself quite ridiculous. Since when had I cared about people so much that I would go this far out of my way for them? I should have just called him a crazy bastard and left this whole thing alone.

To the left of the prayerhouse courtyard, there was a redbrick workshop. The custodian explained that they made tea there, and I nodded impassively. He said that at this time, most of the prayerhouse's residents would be making tea in the workshop, roasting, cutting, carrying, and packaging the tea leaves into tea bags. The custodian took great pride in the tea produced there. Both the prayerhouse and the farm were registered as social welfare facilities. The concrete building at the front was the prayerhouse. The first floor served as both an auditorium and dining hall, and the second and third floors were prayer rooms.

All the small windows were overlaid with iron grates. *Are people here trying to jump out the window midprayer or something?* I wondered. An elderly man was sitting at a bench near the entrance of the building, basking in the sun. He was wearing a green parka too. There was also a young man who, for some reason, was scratching at the wall with his nails. He too was wearing a green parka. Other than those two, there was no one else who stood out. The pair did not react at all as we passed by, as though we were invisible.

The prayer building was exceptionally quiet. The layout of the second and third floors was the exact same, with small doors lining both sides of the corridor. I could not hear prayers from any of the rooms.

The custodian stopped at the very last room on the third floor. There was no visible number, but he told us it was room 309.

"Perhaps you can stay outside of the room?" the custodian suggested.

"Okay."

The custodian and the husband went inside first, leaving the door open for me. The room could not have been more than fifty square feet. Apart from a dirty bucket in the corner, the room was completely bare, with not even a simple table in sight. There was a small radiator, but the temperature inside was no different from the biting cold of the hallway.

Om Tae-seong was lying on the cement floor with a tattered cotton blanket spread beneath him. He too was wearing a green parka. His hair was matted and tangled with dried blood and grease and, although he was not actually bound, he held his wrists and ankles crossed, as if he were tied up. To think he had become so emaciated in just a few months. His fingernails and toenails had turned black and decayed. His once fair and handsome face had disappeared, the color having drained to leave behind only a sickly pallor. An injury from his left eyebrow down to his ear seemed like it would leave a prominent scar. It looked like he had been scratched deeply.

"How is he? He seems to be of the right age," said the custodian.

"What kind of skills does he have?"

"He can roast tea leaves quite well."

"Let's go with this one then."

At the sound of conversation, Tae-seong opened his eyes. His left eye, with the scratched eyebrow, remained shut. His right eye, which he barely opened, seemed out of focus. Tae-seong looked at me for a moment, but then closed his eyes again. I couldn't tell if it was because he was relieved to see me or if he had just completely given up.

What should we do? Should we just let him die? His lack of response was more pathetic than if he had responded by begging to be spared. His was the helpless resignation of a dog on the brink of freezing to death.

I turned away and headed out to the courtyard, leaving the husband and the custodian behind. There was no need for me to stay there any longer. The young man was still scratching at the wall, and the elderly man was still basking in the sun. *Why is he scratching the wall like that? What is the elderly man even looking at?* I asked myself. It seemed like this place only allowed those with disabilities to be there.

Soon, the husband and the custodian also came out into the courtyard. We all walked back to the office. The custodian took off his arm warmers and sat down on the sofa.

"I think I'll head out now. I'll wait for my husband outside," I said.

"It'll be quite cold outside though," the custodian responded.

"I'll be fine."

It felt as though my innards were slowly being frozen with each and every breath. Still, it was better than staying in that office, filled with the unrelenting scent of tea. I stood at the taxi drop-off point looking upon Sodam Farm. To think that something so terrible occurred behind that pretty gate. I had gone too deep. I should have just appreciated the pretty gate from the outside and not gone in.

The husband came out with the tea the custodian had been so proud of. The deal must have gone off without a hitch. We would get Om Tae-seong after a week. I didn't ask how much it had cost. I could not bear hearing a price being placed on a person.

I walked along the road leading down from the farm. There was a convenience store in a small, empty clearing on the mountainside. The two women who had been taking photos in front of Sodam Farm were there, eating hot steamed buns. They seem to be happily enjoying a tranquil winter holiday. They would no doubt be posting their photo to social media. To them, it was just a pretty gate they had stumbled upon by chance. That was the appeal of travel. I envied their ability to enjoy this place. Maybe I should have given them the tea we got from the custodian. Then they could take another picture to upload online and caption it: "So cool! Look at this tea from Sodam Farm we were gifted! We'll be having a cup back at our accommodation—aren't you jealous?"

The idea that this kind of scenario could play out scared me. The Sodam Farm I knew was wildly different to the Sodam Farm they knew. Tea was not the only thing being roasted, cut up, and packaged there. *By all means, sell everything else, but can we leave human beings out of it? We all feel the same pain.*

The husband looked up some Japanese restaurants on his phone. We hadn't planned to go eat right away, but an empty taxi just happened to pass by, and we decided to take it.

Hanging at the entrance to the restaurant was a huge picture of a sumo wrestler. It was like the one I had seen in the Tokyo subway station when I had gone to the neighborhood of Ryogoku for the Ryogoku festival. Befitting the center of the sumo world, there were pictures all over of sumo wrestlers both great and small. Even with the masses congregating for the flea markets and street events, there hadn't been a single trace of litter, as the majority of people had brought along their own bags to deal with their rubbish. This restaurant was as spotless as those streets had been.

The signature dish on the menu here was *chanko nabe*, a superfood eaten by sumo wrestlers to help with weight gain. I ordered the chicken chanko nabe and sipped my warm sake while waiting for the stew to boil. I was starving, but at the same time, felt like I had no appetite. The husband must have noticed it too.

"Wanna start with the *dango*?"

"Nah, they're a pain—too chewy. So, what did you find out?"

"The custodian is Director Jang Mi-sook's uncle."

Our director? Ms. Jang? I had thought our conversation would start with the husband talking about how he had found the prayerhouse and how he knew about their business—something along those lines. I did not expect the director to be mentioned out of nowhere, right from the get-go.

The husband said he had been suspicious of the security guards from the moment he had seen them that night; no security company would sedate people like that. And even in circumstances where it might be necessary, there was no conceivable reason to put someone in a sleeping bag. And on top of all that, the security guards were led by an unarmed civilian woman. Where on earth would you find such a security company? The husband had been watching the whole commotion play out, unperturbed, as if looking upon someone else's house ablaze in the distance. Meanwhile, I had been busy dealing with the flames licking at my own feet, with the arrival of the director. I just thought that the director had come along as well because NM had something to hide.

At any rate, the husband had started his investigations by first figuring out which security company W&L contracted. It was hardly difficult, since it was a service offered by NM. After that, he hired someone from the security company to look at their records and find any incidents linked to W&L. There were several cases reported that year, but that particular day at the husband's place was not among them.

He immediately started to dig up whatever he could about the director. The director was deeply involved in the inner workings of the company. She was in a position where she would deal with any reports that needed to be brought up the chain of command. It would not be too difficult for someone in her position to take advantage of any of the company's blind spots. She wasn't really concerned with mere back-alley spouse selection deals—there was something far more fascinating happening here.

The director's father and younger brother operated a social welfare organization, with her father's facility being based near Gyeonggi-do in the north and her brother's being here, in a city in the mountains. Both these facilities ran the prayer center and a business for the employment of disabled people together. The prayer center in Gyeonggi-do was apparently quite well-known to actual devotees. But there was barely any information available about the prayer center in the mountains. It did not take in anyone who wasn't sent directly from the Gyeonggi-do prayer center.

The husband had acquired most of this information from someone called Elder Choi, who apparently even took people up to the prayer center himself. His actual job was a mystery; all we knew was that he went around different areas in a food truck, which he had remodeled himself to help him in his volunteering efforts for homeless people. The director also sent people to the prayer center sometimes. Tae-seong had been in Gyeonggi-do but was then transferred to the prayer center here. Apparently, people were usually sent here if their condition worsened during the "training" process.

"What kind of training?" I inquired.

"Well, they're probably not honing their baking skills, that's for sure," the husband responded.

I almost gagged as I drank the sake because of how much it burned my throat. The fact that the husband was talking to me like some kind of foreign news correspondent made the drink even harder to swallow. The husband could be the custodian's son and he would just say, *Yeah, that's my father*, as if it were the most ordinary, uninteresting thing in the world. Still, showing any visible shock would seem too dramatic to him. So, I calmly nodded my head in response as I listened. It looked like I could no longer trust the security company. The document I submitted to the director seemed laughable in hindsight. I wrote it while referencing the list of "issues" the director herself had selected. *What have I done?*

"If we're taking Mr. Om with us, we're going to need a place for him to stay," I told the husband.

"We'll just get him a room at a motel to stay in for now."

"It'd be too much for him to stay at our house, right?"

"Why are you being so kind?"

"You never know, he might pay us back the favor one day."

"People don't repay favors to nice people. They only do that for people they're scared of. Nice people? You thank them with words. Scary people? They're the ones you work hard to pay back."

"What a pragmatic thing to say, but it's quite sad when you think about it. What happens if he suddenly disappears?"

"Then that's that. We've already done too much. Why do you keep going out of your way to help him? Just how far do you want to go? Do you want him out of your life or not? Actually, don't even bother trying to be nice. We're just doing what we have to."

"You sound like an insensitive jerk."

"Yeah? And what are you going to do if he mistakes your kindness for love?"

"That would be a problem."

"And that's why I'm telling you to stop being so nice. Women need to be careful. When you're friendly, guys will chase you. When you're kind, they're gonna wanna mess with you. But then if you get mad, you're a bitch. That's the price of being too friendly. Come on, let's go."

The husband got up first and headed for the counter. *That man, he is refreshingly blunt*, I thought to myself. I unconsciously picked up the tea box. The words "Sodam Farm's Traditional Well-Being Tea" were written in green on a white background. The tea was a blend of Solomon's seal, brown rice, and buckwheat. How could I possibly drink this now? I left the box under the table and walked out of the restaurant. I was worried that someone from the restaurant would come running after me with that tea box, right until I got into the taxi.

The hot air of the motel room enveloped me.

"Are you sleeping? You should change out of your clothes before you sleep," said the husband.

My body sank so deeply into the bed that I couldn't even answer him. I woke up later with a burning sensation in my throat. The husband was asleep beside me. I must have dozed off. My tongue felt like sandpaper. I sluggishly began to get out of bed when I suddenly got the urge to go. Great, now, not only was I thirsty, but I also had to pee. I decided to take care of the bathroom first.

After peeing, half-asleep, I looked in the mirror. My eyeliner was smudged, my face was so oily that the bathroom light gleamed off of it, and my eyes were swollen red, as if I had cried myself to sleep. *Someone save me.* Unconsciously, I gripped the sink with all my strength.

It was me. The person lying on the cement floor with a blanket over the body, that person was me. Someone was standing at the door. He was wearing a striped tie and a NM wedding ring. I could not see his face. *Who are you? Honey? Mr. Om Tae-seong? Whoever you are, please, save me.*

He closed the door, and I woke up.

It had all been a dream. I stumbled out of the room and sat at the vanity table, looking over at the husband, who was deep asleep. Why had he agreed so enthusiastically to come with me? What was he trying to prove? Was he warning me that I too would end up in the same place if I went any further?

Thankfully, the prayerhouse with its tightly shut iron gates had not become my grave. Interacting with colleagues who left the company was almost impossible. No one really wanted to see each other. I wondered how they were and where they were now. If someone gave birth to a child that the client did not want, NM paid child support until that child reached adulthood. I had never seen what that support looked like, but I never doubted NM's generous employee benefits.

I wondered what would have happened if Yoo had never come back to NM. Could she have lived a safe, uneventful life? The version of myself I had seen in the dream appeared so wretched. *Someone save me*, I had pleaded. I wanted to fall asleep and dream again. I wanted to get up, open that arched iron gate, and leave. It would be great if I could also just wake up eating hot steamed buns at a convenience store. Those women who were my age had looked pretty.

I needed to get some sleep. The inside of my mouth

felt dry, so I opened the fridge. *What the hell?* Three bottles of sake lay side by side in the fridge. When had he bought them? They were small enough to fit in every outer pocket of his coat, but I hadn't seen him buy anything. When exactly had he had the time to get drunk? What an interesting man.

I took out a bottle of water and drank half of it right there and then. *Ah, I might just survive now.* I lay back down on the bed. It was so hard, but I had been so deeply asleep that I hadn't noticed earlier. Why was I only noticing this now? I lay down on my side, but my shoulder sank in too much, so I turned onto my back.

In any case, I was glad that the husband was here with me. This would have been impossible if I was on my own. *He is the only one I can rely on now. I think I will remember him for a long time.* I forced my eyes closed. I needed to push away that dream from before with another one. I was trying to fall asleep when I heard a loud sound. *BWOMPFF! Geez, that scared me.* The husband's fart made the entire bed shake and, because of the hard plastic mat under the sheets, I felt it too. *Ugh, what a pain.* I slowly got out from under the blanket and pushed it over to my husband before settling in and closing my eyes again. I could not fall asleep.

16

I still didn't know the pseudonym the husband worked under. If I really tried to, I could probably find out what it was, but I chose not to dig.

The husband did all his work strictly in the studio. I never went upstairs, so it never came up, but I was quite sure he didn't want me up there. He never invited anyone home either. He worked alone, in his soundproof studio on the second floor, making the house feel constantly empty.

Once, when I passed by the studio, I overheard him talking on the phone with someone about shares, so he was also apparently involved in some trading. He had three cell phones, and I wondered which one had my number in it. At a glance, the husband always looked carefree; he was never rushing around or in a hurry to get something done. But if you looked closer, you could tell that that he managed his time according to a certain routine. He didn't have the idleness of someone with nothing to do, nor was he carefree in a way that suggested carelessness. He just liked to use his spare time to relax, and really take a break.

The husband wanted an ordinary life with me, and I had to fulfill that desire expertly. As a professional, you had to meet your client's needs with precision, and I happened to be a professional wife. The husband had been working day and night, away from home, for three days since our return from the mountain city. He was working on a new song as a songwriter and producer. Out of the countless new songs that were likely to be released in the near future, I would have no clue which one the husband's was. It seemed like a highly demanding job, so I was surprised that he was able to handle it after everything that happened in the mountain city. He was an intriguing person.

Anyway, I intended to stay oblivious to the husband's job until the end of our marriage. I didn't want to come across a song one day and then suddenly be reminded of the husband; that would be quite awkward. Ultimately, for my own good, I needed to stay out of his territory. With my husband away, and Om Tae-seong coming next week, I thought it was probably a good time for me to go home. I sent the husband a text.

I'm going home for a bit. Hope work on the album goes well.

Okay, see you.

I took the memory card that contained all the pictures I had taken that day with the husband's Olympus
camera, which he had scanned onto the memory card. I
didn't plan on making a photo album as soon as I reached
home, so I left it in my bag. Being at home felt a bit boring now that Granny wasn't around. I didn't even know
who lived next door now.

I immediately threw open the windows to rid the
house of that typical musty smell a house gets when it's
been left vacant too long. I then changed into something
more comfortable. Before I came home today, I had made
up my mind to get rid of the coffee dispenser. I took out
the various compartments from the dispenser and poured
out their contents, and then took the machine to the
lobby. The damn thing was so heavy, I lost count of how
many times I had to stop and put it down on the way.

"I've never seen anyone throw away a commercial
coffee dispenser before."

The building manager wasn't sure what to charge me
for the disposal. He asked me to give him whatever I
thought best, so I handed over a couple of bills and left.
I felt relieved, and like my history could now be di-

vided into B.CD and A.CD—Before Coffee Dispenser
and After Coffee Dispenser. I placed my old coffeemaker where the dispenser had been. I put a sugar bowl
and mug next to the coffeemaker. The ambience of the
room changed completely; it was like I'd moved into a
new house. Since I was already doing chores, I decided
to also vacuum and steam mop the floors. The steam
mop had been given to me by Granny next door, who
had bought it from the young singer oppa.

"I'm good, Granny, you use it," I had told her.

"I have a few more at home. Just take it," she had responded.

The floor sparkled afterward—the mop was definitely effective. Now that the house was clean, I began
to notice the dust that was coming in from outside. I
quickly closed the veranda window and turned on the
heater. I felt completely drained after all the cleaning I
had just done, so I took a blanket and lay down on the
sofa. Nothing felt sweeter than taking a nice nap in your
own home. The clean house smelled fresh and crisp, like
lemons, almost. It was refreshing.

I opened my eyes to the frantic sound of my landline
ringing. My right arm was numb, probably from sleeping
on it. The person on the other end was a salesperson from
a credit card company. How did they know to call exactly
when I was home? They must have been spying on their

customers. The salesperson said they wanted to give me a special offer because I had a good user profile. Their spy must have been a dud, because I definitely hadn't been using my card—I had no time to. Not giving me the chance to get a word in, the salesperson went on and on with their spiel, like they were reading from a manual.

"Look, I'm sorry, but I'm going to hang up now."

"Thank you for talking to our consultant. We hope you have a nice day."

When did I ever ask for a consult? You've just sent my good day out the window. They kept insisting that it was a special offer, but it was just the company pushing their new products. *The bank will pay the fees for you*—did they really think I'd believe that? Maybe they could just put cash in my bank account instead. Then I could make my own payments, without the need for any discounts. But they just kept emphasizing the point about payments, and talking about potential future illnesses.

"So, you're talking about getting insurance?" I tried to clarify.

"No, no, not at all. Also, other than the four major diseases, there are many other illnesses you should prepare for."

"Like I said, you're trying to sell me insurance."

"No, ma'am. I'm telling you, this isn't insurance."

Just because the payments would be made with points didn't mean I wouldn't be paying for insurance. How much would I have to spend each month to get those points? In the end, I would just be spending my own money, so what were they on about? *The bank will pay the fees for you*—yeah, right.

I pulled out the phone cable. It felt as satisfying as throwing out the coffee dispenser. I lay back down on the sofa. Finally, peace and quiet. I closed my eyes and sunk deep into the silence. *Please, just let me stay like this, just for today—one day of peace is all I ask.*

"Hello, neighborhood residents! Call 010-4545-8245 now! Do you have computers, refrigerators, and washing machines that are taking up space and not being used? We are here to help! 010-4545-8245. Hello, neighborhood residents…"

What the hell? Where was this woman's voice coming from?

The voice, which sounded like an emergency announcement from the disaster management headquarters, was echoing from the parking lot. Upon closer listening, it turned out it was just advertising from a used electronics business. Seriously, why was this happening? *I'm raising both hands, both feet. I surrender. You all win. So please, just stop already*, I pleaded.

"Hello, neighborhood residents! Call 010-4545-8245 now!"

Even with the balcony door shut tight, the sound still

penetrated through. I couldn't tell if the soundproofing in the apartment was just that crap, or if that woman had an exceptionally powerful megaphone. What were all these residents with their used electronics doing? *Quickly go get rid of your stuff and shut her up already!* The megaphone woman finally finished shattering my peace and left to solve the concerns of another neighborhood's residents. I could still faintly hear her phone number, "Call 010-4…" I gave up on any rest and got up, folding my blanket.

I filled a pot with water. The fridge was empty; there was nothing to eat. I checked the cabinet where I kept the instant ramen. Damn it, I didn't even have any ramen. I turned off the stove and sat down at the table. I felt even hungrier now that I knew there was nothing to eat. Maybe I could put on the rice cooker and go grab a few things from the market. But then when would I finish cooking, and when would I get to eat? I didn't really want to order takeout all by myself. I called Shi-jeong.

"I'm back home, but the fridge is completely empty. I think I might die of hunger."

"All right, wait for me."

No questions asked, no fuss at all. I was touched. Shi-jeong was coming over.

When I went away on assignments, I thought of her more than I thought of my family. We met as teens, and she was still by my side as we both turned thirty. She was like a nun. I only showed up once every few months, but she always welcomed me back warmly, with open arms and her priest-like heart. Soon after our phone call, Shi-jeong rang my doorbell. She was faster than Chinese takeout delivery. She must have raided her own fridge, as both her hands were loaded with bags.

"Do you have a helicopter or something? I didn't even know it was possible to get here this fast."

"Hush, just eat this first," Shi-jeong said, as she handed me crispy golden cabbage *jeon*.

"You even had time to make jeon?"

"Don't be ridiculous. My mom was already making them when you called."

I rolled up a piece of the cabbage jeon and ate it. It was delicious, still warm and crispy, and it went down so easy, I didn't even have to chew it. Shi-jeong's mother was famous for her cooking and could make even ordinary dishes taste incredibly mouthwatering. She managed to make simple dishes like cabbage jeon, kimchi stew, or bulgogi, which were usually quite predictable, taste surprisingly delicious. She could be a professional chef if she wanted. But Shi-jeong's mother said that if you became too much of an expert about food, it didn't taste as good anymore. None of her children ever fell ill from her cooking, and that was enough for her.

My empty stomach greedily welcomed the cabbage

jeon I sent its way, and after I finished my third piece, Shi-jeong packed away the container.

"We gotta have dinner too," said Shi-jeong.

"Dinner's still a while away."

"I'll whip something up quick."

The lively sounds of cooking could soon be heard emanating from the kitchen. Shi-jeong was maybe not on the same level as her mother, but she did once attend a cooking academy at an advanced level and was fairly skilled. She had a number of skills that she wasn't putting to use. Had she just gone that little bit further, she would have been among the best.

I didn't know what she was doing, but the aroma wafting through the air smelled like the kind of braised short ribs you would get at banquets. I asked her what the smell was, and she told me it was braised oxtail. Her mother had bought the oxtail to make for her father, but Shi-jeong had brought it to my place. It was such simple, childlike thinking. *I should buy him a nice oxtail set and send it to him*, I thought. *Sorry, Shi-jeong's dad, but I am getting the first taste of this oxtail.*

More lively noises from the kitchen followed. Even after taking the steamer off the heat, she continued to clatter around making something. Only after she was done with that did she finally sit on the sofa. I wanted to apologize and thank her with some coffee, but I didn't have any damn coffee. I should have waited until tomorrow to throw away the coffee dispenser. Embarrassed that I didn't have anything better for her, I poured her a glass of mineral water.

"What happened to the coffee dispenser?" asked Shi-jeong.

"Oh that… I gifted it to Granny when she moved out."

"You did the right thing."

"I'll quickly pop out and get us some coffee."

We would likely want to drink more coffee after dinner as well, so it seemed like a good idea to just go and buy a bunch. I couldn't figure out which coffee beans to get, so I just got a pack of eighty instant coffee sachets from a nearby supermarket. Eighty was quite a lot—the instant coffee would turn into coffee beans in our stomachs by the time were through with all of them.

When I got back home, I was greeted by the scent of braised oxtail. Combined with the fragrant vegetables, it felt like a home preparing for a holiday banquet. I was glad I had also brought some beer along. I helped Shi-jeong set the table, which ended up quite full as she had also brought a bunch of side dishes from home. The oxtail she had cooked in the pressure cooker was soft, but chewy. She could honestly go into business setting up a shop specializing in the stuff. It was the real deal. Selling rice cakes was challenging, but this oxtail was really special.

"Hey, Shi-jeong, should I just quit my job and open an oxtail restaurant with you?"

"I'd only cook for people I like."

"I would only let people you like in the front door."

"How would you know what kind of people I like?"

"You like men of the clergy. If I see any Buddhist monks, I'll show them in through the back door."

"I *will* kill you."

Shi-jeong's incredible banquet was our thirtieth-birthday meal. It also felt a bit like our sixtieth birthday, but in a comforting sort of way. We ate, drank, and chatted, imagining what we would be like when we became old grandmothers.

I hadn't had much success making friends like Shi-jeong after I turned twenty. People seemed to keep a set distance, coming together or scattering apart, as and when they needed each other. If someone in the group ever got angry and stormed off, no one would try to follow them and help them resolve things. We could do that when we were younger, but it was impossible now that we were adults. Instead, we just dealt with things by avoiding them.

Plus, it wasn't easy to show all of yourself to someone who didn't share your memories of suffering through growing pains. It was difficult to make people understand why I was the only one saying no when everyone else was saying yes. I assumed that Shi-jeong was probably

the same. She also likely had a hard time explaining why
she chose to stay in faraway hotels when there were usually always motels close by. She hadn't been able to stay
at a motel since Hye-yeong died. "Since when has Jamsil
been in Gangnam? Are you trying to pass yourself off as
some rich Gangnam kid? After all, they love motels too!"
All she could do was laugh in the face of such mockery.
And then she would come to me, because I knew why.

But not everyone who knew about that painful past automatically became a friend. I just so happened to meet a
former classmate from the college newspaper. He had been
spreading gossip about Hye-yeong, so I got sick of it and
put a stop to it. Hye-yeong would often visit our college
and come to the newspaper office to meet me. The only
interactions she and that classmate ever had were short
greetings in passing and that was it. When we met, he introduced me to the others as some high-flying W&L employee, which caught people's interest, and then he prattled
on with all kinds of other nonsense. He told everyone that
I had a friend who had died under really bizarre circumstances. He had only bits and pieces of information he had
heard through the grapevine, but he was out there making himself up to be some kind of expert on the subject.

And then, after all that, he had the gall to ask me if I
knew any nice girls I could set him up with. That's what
friends are for, apparently. *Fuck off, you dickhead. Since when*

are you and I friends? I wanted to say to him. *If you want my
friendship, then come to me with your head bowed, you piece of
shit.* He acted all smug, as if he were some kind of amazing VIP client and *I* was the one chasing him around. If
that were actually the case, he wouldn't need to act like
such a self-important jerk all the time. I had to put up
with his calls for a while: "How's things? Still no news on
those girls?"

He was just your average guy, but he was acting like
he deserved VIP treatment. Who would want to introduce a girl to someone like that? I politely apologized,
saying that our company didn't seem to have what he
was looking for. He should have just signed up properly
as a client and then gotten matches that way. He told
me that he didn't want to pay the fees, that he wanted to
meet girls through me instead. Essentially, he was asking
me to steal client information and give it to him. Where
he got the nerve to ask something like that, with that
stupid mouth of his, was beyond me. Back then, I could
only turn to Shi-jeong, since she knew the bastard too.

"Hey, Shi-jeong," I said, as we lounged on the couch
after dinner, "you know how they say the average life ex-
pectancy is eighty-five? Do you think we'll live that long?"

"Would you like someone to stay by your side until
you die?"

"Yeah, of course, if it's someone who loves me."

"Then I'll stay by your side."

"So, you're saying you're gonna outlive me then?"

"Well, why don't *you* stay by *my* side until I die then?"

I wondered what it had been like for Hye-yeong. We spent good times with each other, so why did she die without us by her side? How did she end up becoming someone we couldn't talk about, couldn't even mention? The three of us first met each other not too long after we entered high school. Shi-jeong walked toward me with her lunchbox in hand. She asked to eat together, and I said yes. A few days later, the same thing happened with Hye-young, and so we became a group of three. Not a particularly exciting start to our story, but we quickly became the Three Musketeers, doing everything together.

Looking back, we were such scaredy-cats, and I think I was the worst of us three. I used to be amazed by kids who spent all their time fooling around, wondering if I too could be like them and just enjoy myself and do what I wanted. My father didn't work at a very large company, but he worked tirelessly as an executive director, right up until his retirement. Even so, he constantly worried about being able to afford the school fees for me and my brother. As for my mother, she only bought clothes once or twice a year, when there were end-of-season sales. They did their best to provide for us, and we never felt like we lacked anything, but we never felt wealthy either.

I used to wonder how long it would take for me to earn as much as my father. I wanted to have a house I could live in by myself, by the time I was thirty. However, when I calculated how much I would earn after I got a job, even renting a single room seemed difficult, let alone buying a whole house. Was I going to end up living in cramped shared housing for the rest of my life? What was the point of me slaving away over my studies then?

The more I thought about it, the more frustrated and irritated I became. But my idea of rebelling only amounted to going clubbing after our exams ended, and I would still show up to school the next day. That cowardly teenager grew up to be the adult I was now, but I honestly didn't think I was any happier than the kids who used to mess around.

I wondered if Shi-jeong felt the same, since she wasn't that different from me. Was she happy now? Why did we seem like such fools?

"Shi-jeong, we're real fuckwits, don't you think?" I said.

"Nah, just you."

"Oh, the nerve, and coming from a nun of all people!"

"Why do you only look at what's in front of you? Put your neck to use and turn around sometimes."

"Oh, let me guess, you're the spokesperson of some contraceptive company, right? Well then maybe you should chuck me some samples."

Shi-jeong glared at me as she stood up to fill the kettle with water. She had started alternating between drinking beer and drinking coffee at some point in the evening. What a strange woman. When we were younger, she used to drink this thing called McCol, some kind of carbonated barley tea that, despite what its name suggested, contained no cola in it. It wasn't even a popular drink, but she would go to supermarkets and buy it by the box.

Sometimes, she would offer me a can too, and I would accept, because everything tasted good back then. But when I found out that she wasn't giving any to Hye-yeong, I stopped taking it. I didn't like feeling needlessly guilty over something so petty.

Ah, right, I was going to make a photo album. It had slipped my mind. I quickly got up and cleared the table, placing the large dishes in the dishwasher and hand-washing the smaller ones. Shi-jeong took care of the leftovers and I wiped down the sink till it sparkled, hanging the dishcloth up neatly after I was done. She made coffee again, and drinking coffee in a spotless kitchen really hit the spot. I knew I had work to do, but it would have been nice if the day just ended there. The dishwasher had already started its rinse cycle.

"Are you gonna get home in time?" I asked.

"Nah, I think I'll just stay the night."

17

We had nothing to do, so I switched on the TV. The news came on, and they were talking about a new variety of apple-melon the size of a baby squash. You could cut the watermelon up and eat it like an apple. It took three agricultural products to introduce one watermelon. But I could see how it would be good for elderly people to carry around because it was light, but it was quite expensive at the same time. The watermelon was supposed to be fruit for the common people. Maybe common people these days had a lot of money, but if that were the case, they weren't really common people, were they? My thoughts got all tangled up. The news story mentioned that all of this year's first harvest would be delivered to department stores. The apple-melon was not a fruit for common folk after all. Shi-jeong debated my observations.

"Do common folk not go to the department store?"

"They do, but are held back because of their wallets. The real department store for the common people is Daiso."

We kept up our useless chatter as we watched TV. Finally, I turned it off. If we went on any longer, I wouldn't be able to make the album.

"Shi-jeong, I forgot, I need to make a photo album for my manager."

"Is making your subordinate do that kind of shit on their break even legal?"

"That's work life for you. All you can do is just acknowledge that it's fucking bullshit and then go ahead and do it anyway."

I plugged the memory card into the computer and printed out the photos. I used thick, pure white A4 paper, the kind people used for presentations. The paper was thick enough not to get soggy even if photos were printed on both sides. I also had photo paper, but it would have been too thick to laminate. There weren't that many photos to print so I printed them one-sided. I spread out the printed paper so the ink could dry. While I brought out the laminator and book binding machine from my brother's room, Shi-jeong brought out the laminating sheets and binding covers. Since we had done this together often, she knew what to do.

"Is 9mm okay for the spring?"

"I think 7mm will be better."

I placed a photo inside a laminating sheet, and Shi-jeong sealed it with the machine. We worked well together, like cogs in a machine. Shi-jeong looked at the photo of the husband we had just laminated. She was suspicious; apparently, he didn't look like someone who worked a corporate job. According to her, if that person was really my manager, their face would bear traces of their struggle to stay alive and stay sane in their position. These traces became triumphant battle scars and made them veterans. Unlike executives at the position of director and above, who no longer worked at the front lines, managers continued to fight on the battleground. Managers also did a lot of client-facing work. The position was just the right level to give clients the impression that they were being treated as important by the company.

I could only imagine how the manager felt, having to pour out drinks during client dinners while making apologies when their superiors were unable to attend because they were "currently away on a business trip," or "busy at a workshop." And sometimes the clients were bastards who, even when received by a manager, sat there with sour expressions, as if they were being forced to drink sewage water. Who did they think they were? If they wanted to meet the higher-ups, they would just have to grow some more and come back another day. It was common for managers to be questioned about their leadership from above, and be attacked with resentment and incompetence from below. At the damn year-end party, where the CEO and board members were all present, managers weren't treated like the executives they were, and were instead treated like the rank-and-file employees they weren't.

The husband's face had no traces of this suffering, something that Shi-jeong could see right away. For someone whose total combined experience in an office job didn't even amount to two years, the bitch really knew her stuff. It was probably thanks to her father, who had worked actively as a director at a public firm for many years.

"All of those executives hiding in their towers are, frankly, useless. On the front lines, the manager is the real tiger," I told Shi-jeong.

"Don't change the subject. It's not easy to look like that at that age. He's pretty all right."

"Want me to introduce you to him?"

"Isn't he married?"

"He's a divorcé."

"Oh, then he's probably surrounded by women. I'm not interested."

"What? Do men get popular with women after divorce?"

"Divorcés just have that vibe. Lots of women are drawn to them."

Shi-jeong finished what she was saying and then went back to laminating in silence, her lips firmly shut. I couldn't understand her. As far as I knew, Shi-jeong had only ever dated two men, each for a short period of time. They were both such short relationships that it felt like too much to even call them relationships. Constantly diving into new hobbies probably made it hard to have a dating life.

Still, I wondered why she so rarely went on dates. Bless her sweet, modest, well-behaved soul. Her mouth wasn't normally very well-behaved though, and she was being unusually quiet today. She looked at the husband's photos as if she were appraising antiques. Then, without even looking my way, she told me to bring the Korean *hanji* paper that we had used before. She said it so seriously that I brought out the box of hanji paper without complaint.

Shi-jeong cut the paper by hand and decorated the photo with it. Soon, a field of cosmos flowers was completed. The once-dull photo became lively. The flowers made for such a beautiful photo frame, and it was almost a waste to simply leave it an album. Cosmos were my favorite flowers, and they suited the husband well.

I wondered what Shi-jeong saw in the husband that reminded her of cosmos flowers.

"What kind of guys are you into these days?" Shi-jeong asked.

"The Gary Oldman type. He's so sexy on a purely physical level that it makes me tremble."

"So if a man like that asked you out, you would date him?"

"That kind of man is sexier when he's someone else's. Why the sudden question though?"

"Just curious. This man isn't really the Gary Oldman type though. Did you sleep with him?"

"I see your disease of just making up scenarios in your head has returned. Okay then, here we go. Have you ever had terminator sex? Let me tell you all about it. This guy will say, 'I'll be back,' just as you think he's finished. And guess what, he really does come back to life, just like that. Pleasure explodes from my body like fireworks. At the same time, wings emerge from his back, spreading wide behind him. And then you go, 'Oh, is it time for you to depart this world? Farewell…' But then! His wings fold back tightly and he whispers, 'I'll be back.' And, once again, he really does come back. Anyway, I don't expect you to know anything about extraterrestrial sex like that."

Shi-jeong smiled slightly and went back to arranging

the photos. I scoffed. *Don't pretend like you don't believe any of it when I know full well you do.*

She made the album cover. Normally, she would finish it off with a simple title, like "Mt. Moonjeong Hiking Club 4.2009." However, this time, she made a man and a woman with the hanji paper and added them to the blue faux leather cover. The simple human figures evoked a wistful and serene feeling. Shi-jeong used the binding machine to punch holes in the photo and align the polypropylene covers on both sides. She then finally inserted the springs and voilà, it was finished. Of all the albums Shi-jeong had made, this had to be the most impressive one so far. As she flipped through the completed album page by page, she noticed that I did not feature in any of the photos.

"So you still don't like getting your picture taken, huh?" she said.

I held my breath, without even realizing. Shi-jeong was about to mention Hye-yeong but I didn't think I was ready. It was difficult to talk about the times we were together, even between the two of us. I also hated the pettiness I still felt toward Hye-yeong, and it kept me from feeling pity for her. I was still angry about those pictures that I was missing from. I was afraid of being linked to a death that was obviously a suicide because of those photos. What if I really was somehow responsible and didn't even know it?

"Yeah, I guess so," I replied, avoiding Shi-jeong's gaze.

The College Entrance Exam Day. I could never forget it, but that had nothing to do with the actual exam itself, and everything to do with the fact that Hye-yeong was taken away from me that day.

We were at a club in Hongdae, downtown Seoul, and while we normally drank beer, Hye-yeong decided to also drink whiskey that night. I couldn't even get down a single glass of whiskey. If I drank too quickly, I'd throw up. But Hye-yeong kept insisting. I would raise my glass, but put it down on the table straight after, to avoid actually drinking. When she saw that, she teased me relentlessly. After that, she danced with any man she could find. I didn't know if it was because I was drunk, but it felt like all the men she danced with just kept looking at me. Some crazy bastard even asked me if I "wanted to get out of here."

I didn't like the crowd, so I wanted to go to a different club. It was getting embarrassing how Hye-yeong was grinding up on and dancing with a bunch of random men. Shi-jeong must've been getting angry too, since she suggested that the two of us just leave. But it wasn't as if we could leave Hye-yeong by herself.

I went over to Hye-yeong and tried to lead her away by the hand. "Let's go."

"Why?" she responded.

"Let's just go."

"Why though?"

"Let's just go, you crazy bitch!"

Somewhere along that process, we broke out into a fight with the men. It started because Hye-yeong suddenly did a complete U-turn and started hitting the man she was dancing with, slapping him on the cheek and cursing at him in a way that really pissed him off. Naturally, he started to retaliate.

I knew Hye-yeong was in the wrong, but we were the Three Musketeers. I started yelling and cursing like crazy. We took advantage of the moment the employees came to help and escaped. We dashed out of the club, running for our lives until we reached the Far-East Broadcasting Station parking lot. Hye-yeong had complained the entire time we were running away, but now that we found a place to hide, she burst into tears. It really annoyed me. It was like she was wailing, *We're over here!* for the entire world to hear.

Two men from the club had chased after us and we could hear them shouting on the main road in front of the broadcasting station. Shi-jeong and I couldn't even

breathe for fear of being caught, but there Hye-yeong
was, crying like a maniac.

"You guys are dead if we see you again!" one of the
men warned and then, thankfully, they left.

"Are you some idiot extra in a horror film? Are you
trying to be the first to die?" I told Hye-yeong. "Even a
child wouldn't cry in a situation like this. Are you insane?"

And with that, I left and took a cab straight home.

We apologized to each other a few days later, but there
was this lingering discomfort I couldn't shake off, and I
wasn't able to be around Hye-yeong the way I was before. From that day on, just looking at her made me feel
irritated and angry. Once I started disliking someone, it
was hard for me to change that feeling. No matter how
sweetly she behaved, I remained unmoved, and I couldn't
hide it either. Hye-yeong could probably tell. She was a
good kid, and it was her first time acting out like that at
the club, so it could have all been laughed off.

I myself didn't understand why I was so angry. I
avoided situations where we would be alone together
at all costs. Even after the college entrance exams were
over and we had more time, I made excuses to avoid
going to the club, saying that we might see those men
again. When she suggested we go out in a different area,
I came up with new excuses.

Hye-yeong had even planned a trip for us to take that

winter break, the last of our high school lives. But I lied and said my parents wouldn't let me go, and the trip got canceled. Shi-jeong and I went to college together and Hye-yeong went to a different college. Still, she would come over to our college. When I would see Hye-yeong from a distance, I would turn around and go the opposite direction. Hye-yeong was no longer my friend. Maybe I had been too harsh with this girl, who was, ultimately, a kind person. Maybe that's why she got rid of all of my pictures.

"I was too harsh to Hye-yeong back then, wasn't I?" I asked Shi-jeong, as if reminiscing, trying to keep it as light as possible. I didn't want Shi-jeong to have to repress her memories of her friend because of me. I was trying to signal to her that it was okay to open up and talk about it. Shi-jeong closed the album and put it on the table with a soft thump.

"If you didn't like her, you didn't like her. It's not like she was that great anyway."

"It seems like Hye-yeong didn't like me much either. But at least I didn't do anything to our photos."

"What happened to the pictures—that was because of me."

"You?"

"I liked you, so I got rid of them. It was way before the club incident."

My heartbeat slowed right down.

I took a moment to catch my breath. In a group of three, one inevitably became the third wheel; that was just the fate of an odd-numbered grouping. In our group, Shi-jeong and Hye-yeong were usually the ones attached at the hip, so much so that I even asked them if they were dating. I didn't think any more of it then; I was indifferent to that kind of thing. Whether they went to the bathroom together, or they left before me to go to after-school tuition, I wasn't bothered by any of it. That was probably the reason our three-sided friendship had maintained its balance for so long.

Why then would Shi-jeong suddenly say she liked me more? Even if that were the case, such petty jealousy didn't seem like reason enough to do away with all of my pictures. Hye-yeong was such a nice person that we felt like we owed her something. She would often make and bring us things, even though we had never asked her to, and honestly, didn't even like all of it. She had once gifted us a pair of childish mittens, knitted laboriously by hand. She made notes in class with so much detail it was like she was writing out the entire textbook. If someone's birthday was approaching, she would start thinking about it days in advance.

As her kindness toward us continued, our feelings of indebtedness grew. We always wondered how she was able to do everything that she did. Did she make time for it all when she took breaks from her studies? Or was this her main focus, and she only studied in the little periods of time she had in between making gifts and planning birthday parties? Was she some kind of genius? Did she ever sleep?

As her friends, we were always on the receiving end. That was also the case for the Coming of Age party. I had felt somewhat distant from her following the incident at the club, but she was being so nice that I couldn't refuse her invitation, especially since she was going to Australia for a working holiday the next semester. It was not so much a party for her going away as it was for us staying behind. She was being so nice to me, but she had already been getting rid of my pictures for a while now by that point. I couldn't believe how childish she had been.

"You both were acting crazy, and I had no idea," I said to Shi-jeong.

"Love is crazy by its very nature."

"And *who* was in love with *whom*?"

"Hye-yeong loved me, and I loved you."

I didn't respond. I touched the laminating machine. It had cooled down, so I turned it off and unplugged it. *I don't know what you're talking about*, I wanted to insist, but my body was under no illusions. *Why deny what you know is true?* it seemed to ask.

It was late and I had to tidy up. I wound up and put away the power cords for the laminator and binding machine, when Shi-jeong came and hugged me from behind, wrapping her hands around my shoulders.

"What the— Can you move? I have to clean up, you know?" I said, and gently pulled free of her clutches. *Calm down*, I told myself. Shi-jeong had always had a habit of clinging on to me like a child. She liked holding hands and was definitely a hugger. Usually, I would just stand still and let her hold me, so pulling away abruptly like that felt strange. *So, Shi-jeong is… I see.* I tried to deconstruct all of the things Shi-jeong had said. When we were freshmen in high school, we both liked this third-year student who was in the Girl Scouts Club with us. We were head over heels for her boyish appearance.

"Hey, Inji, what would you do if she asked you out?" Shi-jeong had asked me back then.

"I'd say yes in a heartbeat! I'd follow her into the depths of hell, honestly."

"And if I asked you out?"

"Be half as sexy as she is, then we'll talk."

When we were in college, I had fallen in love with a senior from Shi-jeong's course who worked on the campus newspaper.

"Hey, Shi-jeong, does he have a girlfriend?"

"He has a boyfriend."

"Ah, you did say he was different. Whoever he is, lucky guy."

"If you're jealous, why not get together with a pretty girl?"

"Is being pretty all that matters? They have to be into me too, you idiot!"

Shi-jeong herself was quite soft and delicate looking, so naturally, she liked macho guys. Or at least, so I had thought. I wasn't bothered by the topic of homosexuality— it was just something that came up naturally in conversations about love. To me, love was a supernatural phenomenon, an intense attraction to someone, without any rhyme or reason behind it. So, even when love happened to flow toward someone of the same sex, it could not be stopped. Who could claim the right to build a dam to stop the on-coming tides? As if mere humans could stop a supernatural force. That was my opinion on the subject.

But I had never felt love toward someone of the same sex myself. Hye-yeong had been throwing away any of photos of me since sophomore year. We were both in the same class then, but I failed the exams that year. Not that it was important. *Oh man, this is all just… So Hye-yeong too? What the heck, what do I even do with this information?*

"Why are you telling me this now?" I asked Shi-jeong.

"I was going to finally confess my feelings to you after the college entrance exams but I couldn't, after what happened that day. Then I was going to tell you on Coming of Age Day, for real, but you remember what happened. Now I'm thirty and I've been holding back all this time—I've gotten quite good at it, wouldn't you say? And I've lost all my sex appeal."

"We must have different definitions of sex appeal. I mean, you probably think your striped slippers are sexier than high heels, right?"

"Huh?"

"I mean, you're wearing them over white socks! It's just…ha! It's fucking hilarious." I laughed.

"If I wear them barefoot, I get calluses and my feet start to smell!"

"Want some coffee?"

I filled the kettle and opened up the instant coffee mix, listening to Shi-jeong as she spoke. Apparently, she and Hye-yeong had been romantically involved for a while during sophomore year.

"You weren't like us," Shi-jeong laughed. I think it was around that time when they were always joined at the hip. I had just thought of them as good friends who would hold hands and put their arms around each other's shoulders. They once kissed while eating ice cream, but I just laughed it off. It was like a little peck between two happy, playful toddlers. Shi-jeong had puckered her lips at me in the same way too. "I'll kiss those lips off of you," I said before pressing our lips together. And yet, I didn't make anything of it. *She's such a sweetheart*, I would just think to myself.

Shi-jeong went on to tell me Hye-yeong deleted my photos after they broke up. In reality it was only a half breakup, since they opted to remain friends in case I found out about them. Hye-yeong couldn't deal with that though. *Oh, that's right! Those mittens!* I suddenly remembered. Hye-yeong had knitted them during winter vacation in sophomore year. They had half a heart on the back of each one. When worn while holding hands, Shi-jeong's and Hye-yeong's would fit together perfectly, but mine did not fit with either of them. Both the shape and the size were different. Hye-yeong said she would find my other half for me and Shi-jeong seemed quite pissed off by that. She didn't wear the mittens; she said they were tacky. Honestly, the mittens were a bit childish, but they were warm, so I wore them anyway.

"Listen, I'll buy you different ones, so stop wearing those mittens!" Shi-jeong insisted.

"Then buy me some. It'll feel even warmer if I have two pairs on."

"Will you freeze to death if you don't wear them?"

From then on, I stopped wearing those mittens out of consideration for Shi-jeong. In hindsight, I realized that it had all been because of me. I was so stupid for not noticing.

"But why did you take the mittens that day at her house? Do you still have them?" I asked Shi-jeong.

"I wanted her to be able to have a proper love story up there, so I burned her mittens along with mine. Anyway, what'd you do with that button?"

"I still have it."

"It's from my middle school uniform, you know."

"You guys are really something. Do you want it back?"

"It made its way to you. Why would I take it back?"

Shi-jeong's button had, after everything, ended up with me. A tiny thing like that could really mess with your head. I handed Shi-jeong her coffee and cleared up all the machines we had been using. I was about to sweep the floor, but I thought the dust might get swept up and land in the coffee, so I moved the machines into my brother's old room first and picked up the scraps of hanji paper on the floor.

"The coffee's great. I love you."

"What are you saying? Move your feet," I said, as I bent down to pick up more paper.

That scared me. It did not sound like something she would normally say. Had she made up her mind to confess today? She really came straight at me and gave me no time to think. But I was sorry for never having realized her feelings for me; it was all my own stupidity. My love was always directed elsewhere, so I had never had time to look at Shi-jeong. Even though it never amounted to a great romance or anything, I had only ever focused on the other side.

Now that I knew, what was I supposed to do? When she was just a friend who stood by my side and supported me with coffee, I knew what to do with her. Maybe I should go get the coffee dispenser back. If Shi-jeong had been a guy, I'd have said something like *You fool, took you long enough* and we would have turned from best friends to lovers who spent the rest of the night getting hot and steamy.

But this is just Shi-jeong… Ah, honestly, this is making my head hurt. What could two girls even do together? Passionately take their clothes off and embrace each other before holding hands and going to sleep? I had already done something similar several times before. In the sauna, we would get fully naked without a second thought and look at and size up each other's bodies. Then we would wash up and sleep next to each other in the resting room. Lovers would do things that were completely different, right?

Love is so complicated. I threw away the scraps of hanji paper that I had gathered and went into the bathroom.

My and Shi-jeong's toothbrushes were hanging side by side in the bathroom. Something that used to be normal looked so unfamiliar now. When my family moved out of Seoul, Shi-jeong brought over a bunch of things.

They were a bunch of small miscellaneous things like toothbrushes, hand towels, mugs, and slippers, but she brought two of everything. I didn't think much of it at the time, but she must have been so excited.

I was considering sleeping on the sofa, but it seemed like a stupid idea, so I lay down on the bed with her. It kept bothering me that Shi-jeong was snuggled up so close, so I quietly shifted away to put some space between us. Was that a mistake? My body was tensed up and my neck felt stiff. I turned my pillow a bit and Shi-jeong spoke.

"You're not gonna get married to that manager from earlier, right?"

"Huh?"

"You're just gonna have extraterrestrial sex with him, right?"

"Yeah…"

"Good night."

Was Shi-jeong perhaps still a virgin? It seemed like she believed that extraterrestrial sex was possible since she had never had any actual experience, outside of watching porn. How did a girl this purehearted like me? I knew a man who had once left me, a long time ago. I also knew a woman who had loved me for an even longer time. The man never came back, but the woman was lying right next to me. Why me?

I looked at Shi-jeong's lips. Should I kiss her? No, I

didn't think I could do it; my body wouldn't move. Shi-jeong was deep asleep. She probably felt relieved, now that she'd confessed. I couldn't believe she was sleeping so soundly after creating such a dilemma for me. I wondered why things had gotten so complicated when we had just started as three friends in a group together. If there had been even one more person, that might have been the end of it.

Shi-jeong also probably felt somehow responsible for Hye-yeong's death. Either way, neither of us had been able to give Hye-yeong what she wanted from us. At some point, we had just shut her out completely. That is not what friends do.

I wondered if Hye-yeong had already started to think the same. What if she killed herself because she had to finally give up on us? I really hoped that wasn't the case. It terrified me. What if "witnesses" showed up, saying things like *No no, two of them were friends, but the other wasn't*? I wondered if Hye-yeong's passing would have been less painful if Shi-jeong had stayed her lover until the very end. It was a love that could not exist in broad daylight, one that would have become much more difficult to sustain, had it been revealed. All because there were people who were trying to shove it into a corner. I wanted to pull that love out and hang it out in the sun.

I wished that everyone could have a nice, fresh, fully

dried-out love. I wished that no one had to cry because of love. I hoped that Shi-jeong did not cry because of me.

When I got up, Shi-jeong had already left, but she had made some refreshing *doenjang* soup and rice before she went. She must have been too shy to face me in the morning after confessing so boldly the night before. I should have at least pretended to be conflicted when she had taken the trouble to make such a difficult confession. But why make breakfast and then run away like a fool?

I ate the soup; it was delicious. All this time, I had regarded Shi-jeong's love as friendship. And now, even though I knew the truth, my body would not move. *Goddamn it, my body seems to have more of a reaction to the soup she made than to Shi-jeong herself.* Feeling both grateful and apologetic, I sent her a text.

The soup's friggin' amazing.

How about you try showing me some of that love.

I stared at her text for a while, then sent a short reply.

I love you so much my heart is in ruins. Happy?

18

The husband came back home earlier than anticipated. The musician he was working with had asked him for an extension. Being a famous singer was a lifelong dream for many, but to this guy, it had become just a job like any other. The husband said the musician sang every song in the plainest way possible, like an old dog that couldn't be taught new tricks. He said that he pleaded with the musician to give it all that he had, as everyone knew he had the ability. It was then that he asked the husband for some more time.

I wondered who it could be. I could probably figure out who it was if I roughly knew their age. The plan was to release just a single for now, and then maybe release a full album based on how sales went. The husband showed more interest in the photo album I made for him than in the album he was producing. Maybe he had kept his expectations low, because I had made it sound like it wasn't a big deal. Shi-jeong's traditional craft skills with hanji and her semimastery of basically everything seemed to have helped me out quite a bit.

"Wow, did you make this with real hanji?" the husband asked.

"Yep."

I briefly explained that a "skilled friend" had helped me make the album. I didn't want to bring Shi-jeong too deep into this world of secrecy and covert dealings. I didn't want to get into any discussions with her about whether NM marriages were good or bad. For the clients who entered these marriages, the traditional system of marriage just didn't suit them, no matter how old and established the system was. Whether it was their only option, or it was just for pleasure, these clients needed NM. However, I didn't like that some of them mocked other people, calling those used to living within the traditional confines of marriage "boring." I didn't think that being traditional was equivalent to being cliché, and there were definitely people who needed the system to protect them.

The kind of love Shi-jeong felt still hadn't been able to break past custom and tradition to enter the system, but at least she didn't mock heterosexual love. She was, naturally, just envious of how openly straight couples were able to love each other. How could love be set within just a handful of frames anyway? Maybe if people lived for about five hundred years each, they wouldn't just live their lives doing the same things as everyone else. With our current lifespans, there wasn't enough time to take a step back or change direction. The only memories we inherited and passed on were those of lives similar to each other's. Any memories of a life lived differently were ultimately repressed and destroyed.

I pitied Shi-jeong's way of loving because she had to figure everything out herself, as if she were the first person like her. I pitied her all the more because I couldn't accept her love. Would things be different if I still had some love left in me? Perhaps.

"Honey, you stay at home," said the husband.

"What?"

"That guy—I'll go pick him up."

The husband talked about it as if it were some simple pickup. I couldn't possibly have forgotten about Om Tae-seong, but I flinched at the sudden mention of him. The husband took the photo album and went upstairs. He was probably going to slip it between some CDs in his collection. This meant that I was deliberately leaving a clear, tangible trace of myself in this house. It was better to do that than to leave traces by accident; those could be stored and used as evidence. I was worried about the FW who came after me, though. Seo-yeon would drop in randomly like before, to make sure her presence was known, and the husband would probably go upstairs with her again. How would Seo-yeon feel if she saw the photo album? *Honey, there's a strange photo album here.*

Oh that, the husband would reply. *My ex-wife made it for me.* It would certainly bother her. It was different knowing about something and actually experiencing it firsthand, with your own eyes.

In the early days of my career, the first thing I would do when starting an assignment was change all the bedding and kitchenware. I didn't want to use bedding that others had slept on naked, or eat with cutlery that had been in other mouths. Now, I just washed and disinfected stuff. I'd come to accept that everyone lived the same way. I didn't know whether I had become lazier or just more easygoing, but I changed and adapted to this new way of life. It wasn't the domestic life that was hard to adapt to, but the people. I didn't know if I just had different blood or maybe my cells were made of something else, but for me, the people were the hardest thing to deal with. I always felt like I was meeting a new species that was similar to me in form only.

Tae-seong was also like that. He didn't seem human. He seemed like a monster who would go home at night and turn into its true form—probably some mushy, slimy creature that resembled an uncut slab of *injeolmi* rice cake—and then change back into human form in the morning. I prayed and hoped that I would never have to deal with anyone like him ever again.

The husband drove his car, which had fully tinted windows, into the motel car park. I waited for him to park, and walked toward him when I saw him get out of the car.

"Have you been waiting long?"

"No, I just got here. What about Tae-seong?"

"He's sleeping."

Tae-seong was curled up in the back seat of the car, sleeping. The husband said he had been sleeping the whole way there. He tapped him lightly on the shoulder, and Tae-seong opened his eyes. It was only then that I truly felt his presence. *That's right, that's what he looks like.*

A small problem had cropped up, which had caused a week-long delay in our plans to pick him up. Tae-seong seemed to have made a considerable recovery during that time. The blue coloration that was spread across his face had disappeared. Sometimes all it took was a haircut and a good scrubbing down to completely change a person's appearance. There was fresh gauze on his wound, which went from his left eyebrow to his cheek. We took him to the room we had booked on the second floor. The place was like any other motel room. There was a small table next to the bed, a fridge next to the dressing table, and a wooden clothes stand instead of a cupboard. The husband had paid in advance for a month's worth of food and rent.

Tae-seong sat on the floor, leaning against the bed. I had packed a simple meal for him, and I set it down on the table. I told him that he could throw away the container I brought his food in, but my instructions fell on deaf ears. Tae-seong just looked wordlessly at the container and rose slowly, moving to lie down on the bed. We left him that way. The owner of the motel was waiting for us at the entrance as we came out to the lobby.

"The man who went up just now is staying here alone, right?"

"He is."

"What should I do if he wants to leave earlier? Organizing a refund would be problematic."

"You don't need to provide a refund. If he wants to leave, just give us a call please."

The husband didn't spare any words of concern or ask that Tae-seong be taken care of. The owner didn't ask us too many questions either. I gave the owner a polite nod and got into the car. I felt a bit better now that Tae-seong was here, instead of in that prayerhouse. I wondered what was going through his mind at this moment. Probably something like, *Why is this happening to me? What did I do wrong?*

I wasn't too sure myself. If you looked at the things he had done, it was all just trivial stuff. Even if I had reported him for constantly following me around, he would probably just have been let off with a warning. But for me, every time I saw him, I would wish him dead. Tae-seong kept bothering me in this strange way where I couldn't face it head-on and deal with it properly.

Apparently, it didn't take much to want to commit murder. Just like a matchstick, which lights up in flames after you strike it a few times, I was ready to kill him if he came to see me just one more time. His repeated visits were a nuisance that fired up my murderous instincts. I also felt wronged, like anyone who looked at us would see a nice, smiley guy on one side, and a crazy woman who kept spitting in his face on the other. Why did he have to keep chasing me around when I wasn't interested, and make me look like a bitch? Was he that clueless? People who were that naive at this age were disgusting in the same way oldies sucking on baby bottles were. *What did you do wrong? We just don't go together, the fact that we even met was wrong.*

The car suddenly felt too warm and stuffy. I rolled my window halfway down.

"Honey, why is it that I get angry just looking at that man?"

"It's only natural. He kept making you apologize and having to make excuses to avoid him. 'I'm sorry, I'm not available today, my apologies, sorry, please leave.' He's the kind of person to bump into you and then wait for you to apologize. Constantly having to apologize and refuse isn't easy. It's different from a simple 'thank you' or 'okay'—it really takes a lot out of a person. If you actually want to form a good relationship with someone, you can't keep making them have to apologize. That just makes them feel pathetic."

I looked at my husband. Was I also going to get as clearheaded as him at that age?

"You're quite handsome, you know."

"I get that a lot."

In any case, I was now going to have to apologize to Tae-seong because of the inhumane happenings at the prayerhouse that I was involved in. I hadn't had the chance to get a single apology from him for what he had done to me earlier, but now I was going to apologize to him again. They very thought made me want to go scream in a field of green onions, where the stalks were nice and tall. *Fuck! What did I even do to you!*

He probably felt like a beggar now, but I was hoping he would rest up and go back to being his original, cheery self, ASAP. *I hope you go back to living a nice life with those people who like you and seem to think you're nice, and never show up in front of me ever again.*

The husband had come back from a studio recording session and was doing the rest of the more technical work at home. It was a recording that had been put off time and time again, so I thought it would take longer. The husband didn't seem very satisfied with it. He said that if he complimented the singer for singing a particular way, he would just keep singing that way. The husband said that he stopped the recording when he did for the sake of the artist. He couldn't bring himself to hit the artist with harsh criticism, when he had tried his best.

There were people who benefited from such remarks, and there were those who didn't. Advice and criticism were not the same. Most people only made harsh, biting critiques as a way of spotlighting their own opinions, while humiliating the other person. The fact that they thought they even had the right to say such things was just narcissism.

Such people used their criticism as a form of catharsis and an ostentatious display of power, just like my mother did. Convincing yourself that the poison you gave someone was actually medicine was nothing but an elaborate form self-defense. Who knew, the victim might come back from the dead and shove an even stronger poison down your throat, tit for tat. *Save me*, you would say. *Take it in and turn it into medicine, it'll only make you stronger*, they would reply. But the husband wasn't the type to just ignore problems because he was afraid his words would come back to poison him. He was just the kind of man who knew his own limits better than other people's limits.

"I can't help him any more from my end," he said.

"Aren't you being too irresponsible as the producer? You should've had more fun with it."

"I'd have a lot more fun if he just died early."

The husband said that even after listening to a handful of verses, it was clear that a better singer would be hard to find, so he was, at least, exceptionally good at singing. But apparently, it was frustrating to listen to his songs, because you would always be waiting for them to end.

The husband said there was no room for the listener to even breathe, because he would sing every word and bar in a long, continuous sequence. Who could it be? This singer sang in a continuous string, as if pulling apart a yarn of wool, the strings interconnected and seemingly never-ending. It didn't matter what the husband said; my mind was full of the names of all the singers I knew. When exactly was an "early" death? I think it would be difficult to call it an "early" death if the person was above fifty. Who on earth could it be? The husband said that singing in that continuous, melody-stringing way was his signature; it used to set him apart from other singers, but now, it would just bore the listeners.

"Is he trying to become some UNESCO intangible cultural heritage or something? He could at least try to sing even one song a little differently. But he just can't do it."

"It's probably just his personal style—you've got to respect it."

"I can't believe it. You both said the exact same thing."

"Really?"

"Yeah, so I told him I'd just go with it."

After that, the husband finished his work on the album with lightning speed. He said that it was like a special anniversary album, released for the singer's own orgasmic satisfaction, so at the very least, it could be used for his own self-pleasure. Whether it would succeed or not was a matter of luck. But what I was most interested in wasn't this mysterious singer, hidden behind a veil of secrecy. The singer's orgasms or luck were none of my business.

What intrigued me the most was the husband. He was talking about his work more often. He kept bringing it up, though he still kept some things hidden. I could never have even imagined this during our first marriage. He would even want to hear what I had to say. "What do you think, honey?" he would ask, but all I would manage to sputter out was, "Hmm, I'm not too sure." What did he want from me? We were together 24/7; what could I possibly tell him that he hadn't already heard?

He was obviously the same man as before, but the husband seemed quite different in this second round of our marriage. He bought alcohol when he was drunk, but apart from that, you would never be able to tell he had been drinking. I bet it wouldn't even turn up on a breathalyzer. I needed the police to give him a fine or something if they saw him going to buy liquor. Or, at the very least, I needed them to say, "You've bought twelve bottles. Your license has been canceled." The husband leaned slightly on the sofa armrest and watched me. I pretended not to see him and focused on folding the laundry I was doing instead.

"Honey."

"Yeah?"

"Honey."

"What?"

"Honey."

"What do you want?"

The husband slapped the armrest, laughing. His face usually didn't change in the slightest when he drank, but his face now was red from the laughter. I was confused— had he choked on his own spit or something? I decided to ignore him. The towels had dried, nice, and softly. The jeans were stiff, as if they had been starched. I thought that folding them in half would leave fold marks, so I decided to hang them up as they were. I asked my husband to bring hangers for the pants, but he said something completely unrelated.

"You've always been the prettiest to me when you look at me like that. When you say 'What?' and turn your head. You aren't too enthusiastic, or too passive. You seem at peace. How do you say 'What?' so plainly? There's no sense of tension in it at all."

What on earth was he going on about? Had the warm turn in the weather toward spring made him all soft? A "what" was simply a "what"—there was nothing more to it. I put the jeans down on the table and called out to him.

"Darling."

"What?"

"Your 'what' sounds quite sexy to me. Let's do it."

The husband clapped his hands, breaking into peals of laughter. *What on earth did that singer do to him?* I wondered. *He's gone mad.* If only he could see how strangely he was behaving in the mirror. And to think that this was the same man who had drawn strict boundaries so we wouldn't get too close. But recently, he had been crossing those boundaries pretty frequently. I think he had a bit more trust in me than he used to.

But I was wary of too much trust. People could use trust as a trap, offering it to you and, once you had grabbed on to it, using it to drag you toward them, effectively leaving you stuck with them. No one was safe from this—it was always just "eat or get eaten"—but between the husband and I, it was clear who had the bigger mouth. I had no intention of biting that crude bait disguised as "trust."

Dear customer, if you do not want to stare at my back for the rest of your life, please clear that bait away. The kind of "take it if you want, or leave it" kind of bait you've left out isn't very nice. I thought negatively of blank checks for a similar reason—complete faith was used as bait in a trap. It was like saying, *You assess things and make the decision, and you take on the liability too. But I get the benefits.*

My second husband was like this. Oblivious to our imminent end of contract, he suggested we live together for a few years outside of NM. He then told me to name my price.

"You can think of it as a blank check," he said.

"Okay, ten billion."

And that was the end of that. I knew the depth of his pockets, so there was no point in pretending to be some oil magnate. If some rich guy wanted to show me what he was worth, the least he could do was lay down a slab of stone so I didn't step in the mud, though a whole sidewalk would be ideal. He soon took back his suggestion.

"If things don't work out between us, will you take responsibility for getting me my money back?"

"Was I the one to make the suggestion?"

"You know, there is such a thing as a reasonable price!"

"Yeah, so stop with the games and just tell me how much you think I'm worth. Then we'll finish this with a simple yes or no. What's so difficult to understand?"

Risk ought to be carried by the person who makes the suggestion. If I happened to say a figure lower than he expected, would he have said that I deserved more? Sadly, the amount he expected was embarrassing to even say aloud. Just for comparison, it was worse than some jerk with a Bentley making his wife travel around on the local subway network. I would rather buy a Mercedes with my own salary.

That fucker. An easy *no*!

On our very last night together, he hugged me, and asked me not to misunderstand him, he was only trying to save me from NM. *I'm sorry, I hadn't realized I had been kidnapped.* I was just doing my job, but it looked like he mistook my competence for actual affection, and was trying to enjoy the same at a dirt-cheap price.

I was so disgusted, I thought seriously about giving

it all up. I set his partner score dirt low on the marriage report; it was a new record. I put in a comment saying that he was a thug masquerading as a gentleman. Since then, I had always made my position very clear. I was a FW. No more, no less. I had no desire to form a deeper connection with anyone, regardless of how much trust we had built up. The same went for love—perhaps even more so. Love made you lose your mind, according to Shi-jeong, which wasn't possible with NM husbands. It would be a conflict of interest.

You're enjoying this, huh? I thought, as I looked at the husband. *Fine. Just stop laughing.* If only I knew who that musician was, I'd go and berate them. *What have you done to him? You know you gotta cut the thread before using it. Why do you string all your melodies together then? Do it differently! Go on, sing the whole song again now, staccato, before I start to really get mad.*

19

I had spent three days going into the office to write out my quarterly report. It was ready on the first day, but I was just killing time. The damn company wouldn't give me anything for finishing it early, and would probably just give me more work to do. They might question whether I had actually put in the effort to write it well. I would also have to deal with the disapproval of my colleagues, who would end up appearing lazy in contrast. So, I was in no rush; I took things slow. Working hard might be good for the company, but what did it get me?

The director had been busy lately, overseeing the field training of two new employees. Two people joining the company at the same time was a rare occurrence. While the company obviously didn't want to keep clients waiting, it didn't hire just anyone. It was for their own benefit—ultimately, the clients were the ones who would have to live with the fledgling hires, not the company.

It appeared that the company had found a bunch of talent in one go this time. New recruits seemed to be getting more and more qualified as the years went by. It wasn't like the company was looking for lengthier and fuller résumés each year; they just hired people who happened to have a long list of qualifications. There were some clients who were dismissive of such employees, saying that a spouse who was too smart, too set in their ways, was exhausting to deal with. That led to some new recruits cutting things out of their résumés so they would be shorter. I was always curious about new recruits. *So, how many degrees do you have?* I would wonder.

I got a text from the director.

Let's get a drink together after work. I have some good news.

How about we talk about good news at work and go home on time, I thought, as I sent my response.

Really? Then drinks on me.

Nope. I'll just put it on the company card.

Okay, I'll finish up soon.

I then sent a text to the husband.

Work dinner tonight.

Suddenly?

Welcome ceremony for new employees.

Take it easy.

Of course.

We went to a wine bar in the lively and rich Samseong-dong, not too far from the director's apartment. I could see the chef grilling fish on a large griddle, and I could hear my stomach rumble. The director seemed to be in a similar state, diving into the appetizer salad and complimentary buckwheat tea as if she didn't plan on eating anything else. The restaurant was apparently a favorite of hers—she even knew where the vegetables were sourced from.

I munched on some cucumber, wondering what the director wanted to talk to me about. Had she noticed anything? She was truly a woman of mystery. The seafood platter we had ordered was brought out. The director lowered her head for a moment and said grace. I was confused; why she was only saying grace now? Was salad not food? Why did she just eat the salad with no prayer? She was always like this, only praying when she felt like it. Phony. The director poured us some wine, and spoke quietly.

"The owner here and I attend the same church. I almost forgot."

The director feared fellow churchgoers more than God. We lightly clinked our glasses together before downing the wine.

"What's the good news?" I asked.

"You, Assistant Manager Noh, have been promoted to associate manager."

Associate manager. This was quite a fast promotion, even for NM. Sure, promotions in the lower levels could be quite quick, but the jump from deputy to associate manager was fairly large. The director requested that I manage the Ace tier. The previous manager had suddenly resigned, which had created an opening. Moving to such a different level from a fieldwork position was not an opportunity that would be offered again anytime soon.

Ace, Platinum, and Diamond—these were the three client tiers at NM. The director was in charge of Ace as well as Platinum, but prioritized Platinum. Black, the highest tier, was managed by none other than the vice president. The Black tier was made up of the crème de la crème from business and political circles. If you were selected as their partner, you received special training. I had also heard that, although an extremely rare occurrence, sometimes temporary employees got sourced externally. I had never met a Black tier member and, even with Ace and Platinum, I never really knew which was which. The higher-ups worried that we would discriminate between clients based on their level, so we weren't given that information. We could only guess from experience.

The author husband would have been an Ace; the current husband was likely Platinum. A member's level wasn't decided based on wealth or fame, but based on NM's own, complicated evaluation system. Ace tiers were rather disposable. They were a good market, but also the source of annoying complaints. There were even instances of dissatisfied members who asked for a refund when the contract was terminated. In such cases the company refunded the client without fuss, and then forfeited their membership. Basically, *fuck off* was the company's response. There were also members who treated field-workers like playthings. If more than two reports were filed against them, then the company gave them a refund without fuss and forfeited their membership too:

You fuck off as well. You seem to have some money, so go use it somewhere else. Members who found themselves booted out would usually throw insults at NM, only to return later seeking readmission.

The conditions for readmission were stricter. You had to pay a readmission fee that amounted to double the money you got as a refund. Still, clients would just accept their fate and pay it. This whole process was also meant to show them their place. The Aces were really quite troublesome, and often caused friction with the selection team as well. When complaints came in, field-workers would blame the selection process, while the selection team would find fault with how the members were managed on-site. *Why did you select such trash?* went one side. *Why don't you know how to deal with clients?* responded the other. Annoying as it was, going through this was pretty much a rite of passage for promotion.

"You can't do fieldwork forever—you've worked for so long as it is. I appreciate all the hard work you've done," said the director.

"Thank you."

"We've worked together for years at this point. Of course I'm gonna look out for you."

The director had been a senior classmate of mine in college. There weren't too many people from our college in the company. The further up you went, the rifer the nepotism, with most of the key positions in the scouting team alumni from the same college as the CEO.

"You can start the new position as soon as you've finished your current assignment. Just hang in there a little longer."

It didn't seem like the director was just offering me this position as a way to keep me quiet because she had found me out. These were genuinely the good-hearted intentions of a college senior looking out for her junior.

If only I hadn't been exposed to the director's other, darker side. I couldn't help but think about what I witnessed at the prayerhouse. What was I supposed to think of her involvement in this business of sending people to the prayer center? Did she not know how people were treated there? How could she be so indifferent? What a frightening person. I shot down the last of my drink almost automatically, without thinking. The director poked fun at me.

"Why are all the kids from our college so uptight? They don't know how to take advantage of their connections. Let's get going."

I chuckled and followed the director to the front counter. The director paid using her company card. The director and the company were codependent, a match made in heaven that would grow old together. I thanked her for the meal. We said our goodbyes, and went our separate ways.

★ ★ ★

Now there was no need for me to return to the office before my contract ended. The husband also seemed to have some free time, since he was done working with that melody-stringing musician who might become an intangible world heritage one day.

He brought out Zalman King's final film from his studio. I tried to buy myself some time by going off to pour us some beer and get us some snacks, but in the end, I could not avoid the maestro.

"Thoughts?"

"The screen is pretty good quality."

Being the musician and audiophile that he was, the husband had installed a home theater system of such caliber that even that granny on the onion patch down the street could probably hear the film. What if she came over with her gardening tools and asked what the hell we were doing in broad daylight? I thought that we should at least lower the volume. However, I couldn't bring myself to speak to the husband while he was facing the great maestro with such sincerity. What exactly was he looking at so seriously? I had never imagined that a day would come where I would be listening to such sounds in this full, three-dimensional surround sound. Just watching porn out in the open like this wasn't really that pleasurable—at least watching it in secret added a certain excitement to the experience.

One of the episodes finished, and another began. *Oh, knock it off! Isn't that food? For eating? Nasty.* I'd rather do that sort of thing myself; watching it on-screen was somehow worse. Just as the main character finished smearing herself with whipped cream, we heard a sound.

"Did the bell just ring?"

"I think so."

If it's that granny with her gardening tools, you're going to be the one to deal with it. However, the tiny intercom screen showed none other than Om Tae-seong. Why on earth was he here? The husband paused the movie.

We had left Tae-seong with some pocket money, in case he decided to leave the motel right away, but he continued to stay there. The motel owner gave us updates every now and then about him, but we had no intention of going there to check on him. Tae-seong was administered meds for bipolar disorder in the prayerhouse, so we did ask if he had any withdrawal symptoms, but that was about it. Either way, he didn't show any symptoms.

The motel owner told us that Tae-seong had been getting along well, and had been very docile. The only thing that perhaps stood out was that he had been requesting an IV drip, so the owner had to call in some unlicensed practitioner. Tae-seong just kept saying that he needed to clean out his blood. He mainly spent his days playing with the motel's dog, and nights watching movies with the employees at the front desk. Tae-seong had spent a month there, and then stayed another week, before finally showing up at our place.

Before Tae-seong sat down on the sofa, he pulled out some honey-citrus tea and whiskey. Although an unusual mix, I accepted it. It was much better than some weird rice cake.

"I'm planning on heading home. I thought I should come see you, so…thank you."

Even if Tae-seong's sincerity was temporary and purely the result of his current situation, I wanted to believe him. And I hoped that this would be the last time I saw him. I wished for him to find happiness, but somewhere out of my view.

We were falling into an awkward silence, so Tae-seong proceeded to try and explain the combination of citrus tea and whiskey. He said that mixing a little whiskey with tea worked well as a cold remedy. Tae-seong had just been to hell and back, but his trivia knowledge and nosy ways remained intact. He looked at the citrus tea and whiskey with an expression of self-satisfaction. Well, actually, he had been *about to* look at them, when his eyes made contact with the CD case of the maestro's work. *Why of all times did you have to come now…?* Tae-seong hurriedly got up.

"I'm going to head off. Have a nice day."

And with that, he hurried off. What an uncomfortable end to it all.

I stood at the entrance and watched Tae-seong exit the front gate. A hint of his former cheeriness was visible, but there was something careful about his movements. He would probably think of me each time he saw the scars on his face. He must have hated me.

This is what our relationship has come to, so let's just never see each other again. I let out a long sigh of frustration and went back inside the house. The maestro's movie was on again. The girl went back to covering her whole body in whipped cream. Maybe I should just drink a whiskey on the rocks and pretend to doze off. I decided not to sit back on the sofa, instead heading for the bathroom.

"Oh honey, don't you wanna watch the movie?"

"I'm just going to wash my hands."

"Want me to pause?"

"It's okay, you can continue watching."

Pause? It's not like the movie's going to be any different once I come back…

20

As I handed in my final field report, I felt like a student who had finished all of her final exams at the end of high school. It was as though I had no clear path forward, but was still going to school, just to kill time. The husband still spent most of his time in the studio on the second floor.

Every now and then, for reasons that I couldn't really understand, he would get excited and come over to embrace me. If I walked around with a towel on my head like some old woman working in the fields, if I was watering the plants with the same look, or huffing and puffing after doing a huge cook up, he would come over, call me "honey," and suddenly, out of the blue, we would be doing it. He sometimes tried to sneak in some position that he had seen in a Zalman King film, but it was usually done quite awkwardly, and I would find it difficult to fully get into it. *Excuse me, sir, I'm sorry but that position is just not working. You're going to break my spine. I've bent so far back it feels like my ribs are going to poke out of my skin.* He didn't realize how weird those positions looked in real life. I wasn't some kind of acrobat.

The husband was still upstairs, for now. I took my coffee with me, sat on the table and looked over into the yard. Lately, even if the grass and weeds grew high, I didn't prune them much. The spring wildflowers bloomed beautifully without my interference. They looked as though they had pitter-pattered down from the sky, rather than grown up from the earth. I liked that the wildflowers looked so casual. The cherry blossom tree was also resplendent, this time with real flowers instead of fairy lights. The falling petals were so beautiful that I would just let them be for a day and then sweep them away the next. I wondered how long they would continue to fall.

I took a sip of the coffee, which had already gone cold, and looked at my phone. I debated between calling and sending a text. Shi-jeong and I usually reached out to each other pretty often, but things had suddenly become awkward between us. *Should I set her up with someone? There have to be some nice girls around.* I was hoping that she wasn't upset that I hadn't called her for so long.

Maybe she regretted confessing her feelings to me. If

I had never known about it, we could have gone on as before, comfortable and casual and cracking jokes together. I decided to just make the call. She answered the phone a bit slower than she usually would.

"Hey, sorry. I was in class. I just stepped out."

"Oh, what class?"

"I've been learning stamp-making recently."

"What? What is that?"

"You make cards with stamps, and pretty little wallets and stuff. I'm planning to start a little workshop if it goes well."

"All right, keep it up then. Let's talk later."

"Hey babe, you want me to send one of the cards I made to your office?"

"What?"

"All right, I'm going back into class now."

Shi-jeong hung up. Had she gone and pressed a stamp into her forehead?

I supposed it was about time to head back in. I scanned the yard. The gate of the shed was a bit creaky; I would have to let the husband know. I had really been filling this bare, unadorned house with quite some commotion throughout my time there. My first marriage with the husband had been quite easygoing, so I hadn't expected this second term. I still didn't know why the husband had applied to renew the contract.

Anyway, there definitely wouldn't be another renewal now. Even before I knew about the promotion, I had decided that I would say no to the husband if he asked for another marriage. We had spent enough time together. We could just say we had spent a hundred years together—it had been long enough; it counted. I didn't think I would be able to forget Seo-yeon. They got along so well that you would think they had divorced as a joke, but we would never know the whole story.

Either way, they weren't obligated explain their relationship or personal issues to other people. I just felt for Seo-yeon, because it looked like she was suffering a bit more. She was a closeted romantic. She ended their marriage, but then wanted to keep him as her man. I wondered what kind of a life Kim had planned to have with Seo-yeon. I hadn't heard anything about an early termination of contract, so I assumed things were going well and according to plan.

In any case, it was all finished now. I felt a weight lift off my shoulders.

It was my last night with the husband, for the second time. I wasn't sure of a lot, but I was sure I wanted to thank him for the whole thing with Om Tae-seong. The husband brushed it a way with a simple "Oh, well, it was nothing." His reaction was like that of a man being thanked for getting takeout in the middle of the night to satisfy the odd cravings of his pregnant wife. So, I quickly put an end to the topic. It had not been an easy topic for me to raise to begin with. With no one else to talk about, now we would have to talk about us. I couldn't think of anything specific to say.

"You know that the garage door is creaky, right?"

"Yep."

"I put the fairy lights in the garage. If you're bored by yourself when winter comes, put a tree up or something."

"Why do you think that I'm going to be alone?"

True, why did I think that? I think it was because of the emptiness that constantly hovered over the husband. He wasn't the type of person to become obsessed with people. In fact, he had always been more attached to objects such as game consoles, cameras, and CDs. There were times when this house seemed like the husband's safety house. He seemed fine with this lifestyle, and being alone seemed to suit him. I didn't want to get in the way of his solitude. If it bothered me and I went upstairs to try and talk to him, I would be irritating background noise, like the woman's voice over the megaphone: "Hello, neighborhood residents! Call 010-4545-8245 now!"

I flattened the center of my pillow and laid my head down on it, ready for sleep. Going to bed early was a good idea if I wanted to be able to wrap everything up by noon tomorrow. I pulled the covers up.

"Honey, if we meet again, let's just live together," the husband said.

Oh my, it looked like my dear client was looking to renew our contract again. *Excuse me, you aren't the only one who gets to have all fun of choosing a partner.* People had no idea how exhausting it was to be paired with a husband in the arts back-to-back. I would rather just meet such men through their artworks. To meet them in real life was exhausting. They had complicated, knotted souls, rather than free-spirited ones. If you wanted to keep these men somewhat sane, you had to remain unmoved despite the crazy things they might do. You basically had to be a re-incarnation of the Buddha. One more round? I needed to tell the director to hand over her secret list of ace FWs to him. *I'm sorry, you don't seem to be aware of this, but we have a number of stunningly beautiful field wives for you to choose from.*

"Why do you say that?" I asked.

"It's fun, the way we keep meeting. You know, we met at the club that time. The day that you took your college entrance exams."

I was beyond shocked. *Wait. Wait a minute! What?* I kicked off the covers and stood straight up. My desire to sleep disappeared entirely. That day, those guys had been a mob of rowdy idiots. The husband had been of those dickheads?

"I didn't realize at first either, I just thought you looked kinda familiar. After we split up for the first time, it suddenly came to me. I was like, *ohhh, it's her.* The girl who wanted to have her cherry popped as a postexam ceremony."

"What? Me?"

"I know it wasn't your idea."

We would have been nineteen, and the husband, thirty. We were at the age where we were out to have a good time with no idea what that even meant, but the husband was at an age where he knew exactly how to have a good time. He was at the age where he could give a smile to Hye-yeong, even when she danced senselessly toward him. He said he bought us a round of beer to congratulate us on finishing our exams, though I didn't remember that.

Anyway, it was at that time that Hye-yeong pointed toward me, and asked him to help me lose my virginity to celebrate finishing my exams. According to her, I was too embarrassed to ask, so she was doing it on my behalf. For every generation of adults, teenagers were very mysterious entities. If you were too preachy, and gave them too much unsolicited advice, then you were immediately labeled a stubborn old *kkondae*—out of touch and self-important. If you left them alone, they would make all their mistakes, grow in the ways they had to, and just find their own way. But still, sex to commemorate the end of exams was going a bit too far. Trying to get the stress of the exams out of your system by losing your virginity was way too reckless. No matter how immature you might be, being so careless about your first time just wasn't okay.

"Just have your fun and then go home, kid." The husband turned Hye-yeong away. But his friend kept looking at me, seemingly having received the same request to bed me from Hye-yeong. The husband said that I had seemed like a strange kid too, because I was partying in too carefree a manner for someone who had asked her friend to do something so absurd. I wasn't interested in the friend who was going around making requests on my behalf, too busy being silly and cracking jokes with the other friend standing in front of me. I did look like quite carefree and happy, like I'd just finished my exams, but I didn't look nervous, and gave off no indication that I was looking for sex.

So why is that other girl going around saying that? he had wondered. He had no intention of casting doubt over our friendship, but it seemed clear to him that I was in danger. The husband told his friend to call Hye-yeong over again. He meant to take her out of the club and send her home.

"I'll take her."

"Okay, but not the girl in the zip-up hoodie," Hye-yeong interrupted, and the husband's friend seemed displeased with Hye-yeong's words.

"What, is she a guy wearing a skirt?"

"What are you talking about?"

"Whatever, I don't know about her but *you* come with me."

As they were leaving, I latched on to Hye-yeong's arm. Without any warning, Hye-yeong suddenly slapped the husband's friend in the face. He yanked Hye-yeong's hair. If the staff had not intervened, it would have been a trip to the police station to commemorate our completion of college entrance exams. The classmate stalked us all the way to the front of the broadcasting station, fuming with rage. He was able to find us hiding in the car park because of the sound of Hye-yeong's muffled crying. But he disappeared after hurling a few insults. We felt extremely fortunate to have escaped that situation.

I was entirely unaware that the husband had traced his friend's steps and told him off quite angrily. Until now, I had just remembered him as one of the two scumbags who harassed us that night. What a small world.

The husband laughed heartily after hearing my story, "So that's what happened with you guys that night." I now understood why Hye-yeong had apologized to me so profusely. She was a nice girl overall, so I didn't take her off-putting, prolonged apology too seriously. I could never have even imagined the real reason she was apologizing.

In any case, I had started to dislike her after that day and just pretended to accept her apology. I couldn't quite fathom why Hye-yeong had done that though. Had she wanted to prove to Shi-jeong that I was a woman who had sex with men? Love was so cruel, and so stupid. The husband opened his mouth to ask me a question.

"So, what is that girl up to nowadays?"

"She's dead."

"She did give me an uneasy feeling, like I should be worried. What about the one who was next to her, how is she?"

"Yeah, she's doing well. You have a good memory."

"I remember you did some strange kind of dance."

"How dare you! When I danced, everyone only had eyes for me."

"I'm sure you're right," he said with a laugh.

So that was why he wanted to re-sign the marriage contract. He wanted to momentarily return to the vivid, nostalgic memories that had come flooding back to him. He wanted to go back to who he was before he was someone's man, in a relationship or in a marriage, but after he had already overcome his difficult, painful past and wouldn't have to go through it again. Ironically, he had wanted to experience marriage one more time, even if it was through NM.

The fact that fate had brought us together again had excited the husband too. He said that Tae-seong's appearance had felt so ridiculous, it had made him laugh in disbelief. He had never intended to, but he had been by my side every time I was in a crisis. Once when I was nineteen, and once again when I was twenty-nine.

"I guess you'll show up again when I'm thirty-nine."

"Please, for the love of God, have some other guy with you when you're thirty-nine."

"Why?"

"It's gonna be embarrassing for me if it's something that I can't deal with for you."

This guy sure did have a cute side to him. It seemed like I might see him again in ten years. I shifted the quilt over to the side. I wanted to show him how much more thrilling real life could be than a movie. The husband began taking off his clothes, and I took it as a challenge, rushing to get mine off as well. He finished stripping slightly ahead of me, then began to help me, taking my bra off.

"Remember the exam day? Let's make up for what we didn't do then."

Why hadn't he said so earlier? If he had, I probably would have approached things with a bit more than just professionalism. The husband *really* made up for everything. It seemed like he had finally figured out how to do the things he saw on-screen. I was in a daze, like a passenger on a flight that just took off, with no buildup or warning. The plane seemed to keep revving up its engines until it reached a stable flying position. I felt something inside me. Gentle yet intense. I had never felt fireworks like that go off across my body. *God help me.*

"Are you all right?"

"Yeah."

"We can take a break if you're tired."

"No."

My God. I might just hear the "I'll be back." Those angel wings really could appear behind him after all. This heavenly sex was our last; we would disappear from each other's lives after this. We both knew it, so we didn't talk about it. If we were fated to meet again, then we would—if we truly were connected by fate. The husband had finished rising in elevation to a safe altitude and began flying level. I unfastened my seat belt and began moving. I signaled to him to wait for a minute, and pulled away momentarily to go sink down between his legs. I took his cock into my mouth for the first time. I never knew he would like it so much; why hadn't he said anything sooner?

"You like that?"

"Very much."

21

I completed my assignment and was given a week off. It wasn't paid leave, but just some time for me to rest before I returned to work. I hadn't informed Shi-jeong yet; I needed some time, but it wasn't because of her. I had been thinking about my career. If someone were to ask me how my twenties were, I would struggle to give them a proper response.

They might look at my suitcase and ask if it was for travel. An understandable assumption. *It must be nice to get to travel*, they would say, only to hear me mumble, *Yeah...kinda*, in response. My twenties weren't what I had wanted them to be when I was in my teens. And now, I was already thirty. I didn't want any more regrets when I left my thirties behind. I had been carrying around this big trunk with me, cramming my life into it bit by bit, and it was time for me to throw it away. A single gold button that I could firmly grasp in my hand was the only possession I needed now.

I wrote out my resignation letter and went to the office. It seemed like the director thought I had come to work with that promotion in mind. It was, without a doubt, a good position when you considered all the benefits.

As I arrived at the office, I hesitated for a moment. Was this just an impulsive decision I was making because my last contract had me feeling stuck? Now that I was about to hand in my resignation, the company didn't seem all that bad. Where else would be better? The manager of the Ace tier, who oversaw our department, had also recently resigned and gone elsewhere. What if they had taken away critical information, and our company suffered as a result?

Suddenly, I was getting emotionally attached. In the glass-walled conference room, the director was talking to two new hires. These kids weren't like us back in the day. They lacked the drive. The director seemed to be discussing something important, but they just stared at her blankly. The director and I made eye contact. She gestured for me to come in. I entered the conference room hesitantly, and the two new hires immediately stood up. The director introduced me as the new manager.

"Good to see you. Please have a seat," I said to them.

"No need to sit. Ms. Shin, have a think about it and let me know by the time you leave work today, all right? Go on, you can go now," the director said.

They looked almost cute, greeting us in unison and leaving as per the director's instructions.

"Are they still in training?" I asked.

"No, they're in their probation period. But the little one, Shin Seung-ha, got a marriage proposal already."

"Isn't that too soon?"

It was still early days—they needed to spend some time talking to their senior colleagues, getting come secondhand knowledge, and building their self-esteem.

"Manager Jang took a few employees with her when she left. They all suddenly started submitting their resignations and then, they were gone. That's why I put the two new hires on the waiting list—there was a staff shortage. But marriage proposals started coming in almost immediately. So, I'm worried. Jang and Director Song of the scout team, they were close. When I asked the company to watch them, no one really listened to me. And now, I'm the one running around, trying to put out fires. Give me a minute, I have to go upstairs. We can discuss the rest over lunch."

The director left the conference room. The company suddenly felt more exciting. If I submitted my resignation, it looked like I would also be joining Manager Jang. What eerie timing. Maybe I could just stay for one more year.

But then again, that's what I had told myself when I joined, but that one year became seven. Time really just flew by. I happened to have received training in this very conference room. I had joined with a sense of resignation, and was quite ambivalent during training. They said it was a training session for field marriages, so I thought I'd be learning some sex techniques. But the director's words took me by surprise.

"I don't know what the scout team saw in you. But I do know that the second you start acting like a prostitute, you get fired."

Lowering the company's credibility meant immediate dismissal. There were lots of other avenues for people who wanted prostitutes. The difference between marriage and prostitution is that during marriage, sex wasn't the goal, but just a part of life. The director always made a point of emphasizing this.

"But I know some people who get married for that very purpose," I said at the time.

"Yes, but they call it a marriage—they don't say they've hired a resident prostitute, do they?"

Sex within marriage wasn't an act that could be quantified by money. It was one of the areas where NM's marriages differed from conventional ones, since an NM marriage required a significant amount of money. In exchange, members could actively participate, for a set period, in the kind of married life they had always desired.

The reason the director emphasized the difference between prostitution and NM's work, right from the start, was because it was the part that worried new hires the most. Since marriage did involve sexual interactions, some anxiety was unavoidable. In cases of severe anxiety, an asexual spouse would be assigned as their first. In other words, if you so wished, you could have a job without any sex until you resigned. Asexual or sexless groups were classified separately, and they had more members than one might think. Occasionally, people would come to NM when they wanted to hide their sexuality. The marriage would be like a facade, meant to show the world that they were in a live-in relationship with someone of the opposite sex. At least people weren't *as* averse to such relationships as they were to same-sex ones. Some marriages were sexless too, but many field-workers preferred to avoid those. A junior colleague living a sexless life came to the office once to lament their fate.

"I have no pleasure in life," she said.

"Use toys then."

"What if I do, but then get caught?"

"Don't underestimate the contents in your fridge. There are a lot of objects out there that are better than your husband."

Such was the director's wise advice. This was the kind of education we got—an education meant to minimize our emotional strife. "At home, don't just stand around like you don't know what to do. Always act as if you just got back from the market, or got home from work." And if our husband started to think that they hired a prostitute, we were to quash that misunderstanding immediately. Small talk like "Hey honey, open this window for me" was the most effective, she would say.

"You shouldn't try to change yourself. Whether your husband is in his twenties or a hundred-year-old grandpa, he chose you for the way you are right now. This isn't a company that sends out wives cut uniformly out of some matrix. Most important of all—don't fall in love. Save that for somewhere else."

The director concealed the fact that we had been in the same college until I became a section head. If I resigned too soon, she would have given away her information for nothing. Not only were we from the same college, but we had actually been in the same department, which made me her direct junior. I was well aware that the director had been looking out for me all this time, even when I used consecutive no's. With a different FW, the disciplinary action would have been much harsher than just writing a report. The director was my only saving grace; she just pretended to look the other way. Still, I didn't get any promotions, since the other superiors were watching me like hawks.

"That other director cracks me up," she said, about another superior. "Why did she pick you for fieldwork? She lets her juniors just sit around doing desk jobs. Well, if this is how she's going to act, then I'm not going to just sit around either. I'm going to send all of her juniors off to the highlands."

Among ourselves, we jokingly referred to the most troublesome Ace tier members as "the highlands." Anyway, that was how the director looked out for me. That was why I was all the more disappointed about her involvement with the prayerhouse. I really wished I could keep seeing her as a good mentor. I started my first day at work in this conference room, and this was where I was going to finish. I sent a message to Kim.

I'm resigning today.

You're leaving, huh?

Make sure to go for that promotion this year.

This company is nuts. Farewell.

I also sent a message to Yoo.

I'm resigning today.

So, you're going back home?

Yep. If the window's too big, it's hot in the summer and cold in the winter. You know what I mean?

Yep. Thanks for everything.

Did your father come looking for you because your salary was reduced?

Yeah, he did, but the director handled it well. He left all my banking slips, the cash card, and even wrote an agreement saying he won't come looking for me again.

That's good. Do you feel better now?

I'm not sure yet.

I understand. Anyway, enjoy the rest of your assignment.

I left the conference room and went to the director's office. I placed my resignation letter, employee ID, and the company-issued cell phone on her desk. *Take care and farewell.*

It would take a bit more time to tell whether my life at the company had been a good one. After all, if someone regretted their life, it didn't necessarily mean that they didn't live it right. Having experienced life with many people, I had become somewhat more forgiving. I could tell, because I'd started communicating with my mother and checking in on how she was doing. Was it possible to forgive someone who didn't realize what they had done wrong? Well, in the eyes of my mother, I too was someone who didn't understand what I had done. We both might have to learn to coexist without ever making it to mutual understanding or forgiveness. Love looked very different to my mother and me.

When I was in college, I got into the college newspaper thanks to a senior who I had a crush on. Being close to him and being part of something with him felt good. I did all kinds of odd jobs, from planning journalism projects to production, as well as taking care of all the little things, including his meals. The people at the clubs were quite strict about things, so if they said we were going out, we had to go out, and if they told us to drink, we drank without fuss.

At the time, I was in a headspace where I was all *to hell with it all, fuck love and everything else*, and that was when I started getting close to the senior. He kissed me and we soon became a couple. My mother's objections didn't matter. I didn't want to tailor my man to my mother's tastes. We didn't even care too much about having a big, traditional wedding. For me, even just having my belongings at his apartment was enough. We were genuinely happy, and were going to have our own private wedding with just the two of us, when he suddenly disappeared a few days before that.

"I sent him away," my mother told me.

My mother considered my partner's disappearance an achievement, the outcome of something that had been a challenge for her from the start. We thought that we had overcome it, and were confident that we would continue to do so going into the future. If he was the kind of person who would suddenly leave, we wouldn't have started in the first place. There had to be a reason.

In the aftermath of his disappearance, I didn't want to argue with my mother. She truly believed that she had the right to judge a person's inherent, intrinsic identity. In the face of such arrogance, I had nothing to say.

"He's neither this nor that, which makes him even dirtier," she said.

"*Even* dirtier?"

"Men who lay with other men and then touch my daughter—it's unforgivable."

"You seem to know a lot about men laying with each other. Why is that dirty? Is a man's penis only clean when it enters a vagina? Well, I actually prefer it coming in the other way, Mom, that's what your daughter's like. So don't talk like that about others."

I was my senior's first woman, meaning that he realized he was bisexual because of our relationship. It was because of me that he became one of the "even dirtier" people my mother scoffed at. When we started dating, he went through another identity crisis. He even stopped going to the gay club where he had close friends. It seemed like he wasn't receiving a warm welcome there anymore either. It was just like the kind of discrimination straight people perpetrated. It seemed like discrimination existed in that world too.

I didn't think he left because he no longer loved me or because of my mother's opposition. He had always wanted to find himself. His journey was perhaps getting too long. I hoped he came to find me some day, and explained that he now understood why he had left.

Perhaps he would even ask me, with a smile, if I thought it was kinda cute that he had just disappeared like that.

I chose to work at NM because of the opportunity to go on long business trips. I liked the idea of not having to face my mother every day, even if it was because of work. My mother didn't oppose it either. She seemed to think anything was okay, as long as it wasn't life with my senior. I was also okay with anything, as long as it wasn't life with my mother. Now, I was leaving the company. I wanted to focus more on myself. Before going home, I called Shi-jeong.

"How are the stamps going?" I inquired.

"I'm also making tote bags these days."

"Okay, let's set up a workshop together then."

"What about your work?"

"I quit today."

"Oh, good for you. Your scrapbook albums will look much prettier with stamps in them. I'm also learning ribbon crafts right now, so we can also wrap gift boxes. Will you be home today?"

"Yeah, come over after you finish."

"I'll bring some of the things I made. I love you."

She was truly insane. Shi-jeong hung up the phone first again. Maybe I shouldn't have suggested doing a workshop together. I was already worried about being stuck with her all the time. There was no right answer to dealing with her. My severance pay wasn't much, but if I combined it with the money I'd saved up, we would probably be able to set up a workshop. And if it didn't work out, I could just tell her to make tteok cakes. And if that didn't work, she could go back to drawing webtoons. And if none of those worked out? Well, that was something to worry about then. I was sure Shi-jeong would learn something new in the meantime.

I went grocery shopping. Shi-jeong liked chicken, so I planned to make a braised chicken dish. She also liked tofu, so if we made both, we could have a real hearty meal. Standing in front of my door with my shopping basket in hand, I glanced at the neighboring apartment. It was quiet. I wondered who lived there. I often tried to listen through the wall, to fulfill the information-gathering "mission" bestowed upon me by Granny, to see if they were hammering in any nails. I couldn't hear any sound at all, let alone any hammering. At least there wouldn't be any dead people.

I put in the key code and entered the apartment. The suitcase I had left in front of the shoe rack had been there for some time. I had meant to throw it away a long time ago. It reminded me of my mother more than NM. When I was still a trainee and unsure about whether to stay at NM, she was the one who persuaded me to stay.

"You were in a pile of shit. A filthy mess that no one wanted to touch. I did what I did because I'm your mother. You'll know better when you start working. Go, see how men and women go about things."

I didn't think twice about love being sold in such a dirty way. My time at NM was longer than expected. The more time passed, the harder it became to leave. Leaving for a while would only result in returning.

People around me only cared about the person I was seeing. No one asked if I was happy. And no one was interested in my unhappiness. Even if I said that I was having a hard time, it was useless to argue. *Why? What do you lack?* Perhaps I was angry at such indifference, and venting my anger only made things more difficult for me. Now, I was thirty years old, but I still didn't have a precise sense of being. I did, however, feel a kind of flexibility, so to speak. *What's the problem? I like living like this!* I might say. Why couldn't I have been more flexible back then? I wanted to live better now.

I started boiling the chicken. I then rinsed it with some water and put it back on the stove garnished with potatoes. It was a method that Shi-jeong had taught me to remove the chicken odor. Wait, where were the glass noodles? They needed to be soaked first. I dissolved the seasoning sauce first before starting a search for the noodles in the kitchen cabinet. I had never attempted this dish, so it was quite demanding. Like, when was I supposed to season the mung bean jelly? Shi-jeong could cook several things simultaneously, but I struggled with even just one.

Ah, right, rice, rice, rice! I had forgotten to cook the rice. I hurriedly washed and set the rice to cook. Where was this ribbon craft class that Shi-jeong was attending anyway? She had mentioned a place. She was the type to spontaneously get on a rental scooter and be here the next minute if she felt like it. I wanted to set up the table all nice before that.

Just then, the doorbell rang, multiple times. *Wow, does she really have a private helicopter?* I put the brass bowl in the sink. "Just a second!" I shouted, then quickly pulled out a bottle of McCol from the refrigerator and placed it on the dining table. Shi-jeong would be surprised to see a drink from our teenage years. I wanted us to have a nice, refreshing drink and go back to the good old days for a bit. *This time, I'll be the one to give you some McCol.* I rushed to the front door.

"Hey, you know the code to get in, so why—"

A tteok cake. I saw a tteok cake staring at me through the now-slightly-ajar door. There was no one there, just the tteok cake, in a box, with a yellow Post-it note attached. "I just want to know why you hate me," read the neatly written message.

That crazy son of a bitch.

I quickly closed and locked the door. I could feel my energy draining from my body. I stumbled backward, my foot catching on the suitcase. Instinctively, I grabbed the handle. What should I do? Memories of the husband and Shi-jeong began to simultaneously surface in my mind. Would it be safer to go to him? Or should I call Shi-jeong first? *Why am I so powerless?* Nausea and dizziness washed over me. A silence violently erupted around me and I felt a disorienting quietude descend. The tranquil quiet I had longed for had finally come, but instead of providing solace, it enveloped me, like a veil over my eyes.

★ ★ ★ ★ ★

TRANSLATOR'S NOTES

Translation is often likened to navigating a boat across a river. In translating *The Trunk* by Kim Ryeo-ryeong, the KoLab members embarked on a linguistic odyssey, striving to faithfully convey the author's distinctive wit and the intricate emotions embedded in her narratives about human relationships. This journey challenged us to preserve the essence of her keen insights into the wounds and dilemmas intrinsic to human connections.

Our odyssey was a collaborative venture, far from a solitary pursuit. We were joined by thirteen steadfast companions: Yoon-kyung Joo, Violet Reeves, Kiah Greenwood, Sunny Kandula, Cheyenne Lim, Keith Wong, Daniel Gage-Brown, Sneha Karri, Mimi Lee, Vienna Harkness, Injee Nam, Jamie Lim-Young, and especially Aditi Dubey, who played a crucial role in diligently refining the final drafts. I owe a debt of gratitude to each of these individuals for their invaluable contributions.

Special thanks are due to Dr. Adam Zulawnik, whose dedicated leadership was indispensable. Without his tireless efforts and guidance, completing this project would have been impossible. Additionally, the contributions of Mr. Tony Malone, who reviewed our drafts, were invaluable in enhancing the quality and accuracy of our translation. Finally, heartfelt thanks to Changbi Publishers and HarperCollins, whose active support in translating and publishing this work was essential.

This book marks the beginning of what we hope will be many more such "KoLab"orative adventures, inviting more individuals to join us in the thrilling journey of translation. We hope this project inspires others to experience the joys of translation and of reading Korean literature.

—Yonjae Paik (Australian National University)

When I first read *The Trunk*, it surprised me. A blend of romance, suspense, and social commentary, it made for a very interesting read. The process of translating it into English was also surprising in many ways. There were the regular problems of syntax and semantics that come with trying to bring ideas from one system of language into another. However, there were also the unexpected challenges and joys of writing as a group, and of learning important translation practices while implementing them. Faithfulness is a tricky idea in translation, and I do not know whether ours is a faithful translation, but I do think it is a sincere one. I am grateful to my fellow collaborators for their intelligent insights and diligent efforts.

This project presented a unique opportunity for its participants, many of whom (myself included) are not professional translators. A different project with similar goals might have had several barriers to entry, but we were asked for nothing but our commitment and hard work. I am very grateful to the institutions that made this project possible, and to Dr. Adam Zulawnik for being such a dedicated teacher. Special thanks to Dr. Paik Yonjae, whose generosity and support have been enormous and invaluable. I give my thanks to the many people who constantly inspire and encourage me, and my apologies to any friends, family, or PhD supervisors I may have neglected while I spent hours on a project I forgot to mention.

—Aditi Dubey (Australian National University)

South Korea faces a demographic crisis with the world's lowest fertility rate, which could see its population of just over fifty million halve by 2100. Young people are increasingly either choosing to not have children or are simply not interested in amorous relationships, not to mention marriage, the latter of which, in a traditionally conservative country, is seen as a prerequisite for child-rearing. Kim Ryeo-ryeong's work, set in the near future, questions the so-called "sanctity" of marriage. The world described within already has precursors in our time, with the likes of rent-a-friend and rent-a-partner services in South Korea and Japan.

The English translation of *The Trunk* is the result of an intensive literary translation workshop, Novel Translations: A Korean-English Literary Odyssey. With my supervision and "guidance" (as we are all continually working to become better translators, me included), thirteen talented university students from across Australia collaborated on highly demanding cross-cultural translation. The translation of Kim's novel was a real "literary odyssey," worthy of the workshop title. What you read is the outcome of hours upon hours of painstaking work only made possible because of the immense passion for literature demonstrated by the participants of the workshop.

I would like to thank, first and foremost, HarperCollins for arduously editing our final draft work, and Mr. Tony Malone (*Tony's Reading List*) for much-needed feedback on the first draft. I extend my most sincere gratitude to Dr.

Yon Jae Paik (Australian National University) for taking initiative in putting together the workshop, applying for and successfully securing funding for the project, and for kindly inviting me to take part. I would like to thank the Literature Translation Institute of Korea for its generous funding support and continuous work to promote Korean literature overseas. Thank you to the author of the book, Kim Ryeo-ryeong, for her creativity and for bringing such a relevant and engaging tale to the world. And finally, last, but certainly not least, I want to sincerely thank each and every one of the participants of the workshop, the KoLab team (listed elsewhere), for their fabulous hard work and understanding during all those late evening hours.

—Adam Zulawnik (Asia Institute, University of Melbourne)

May 2024